THE ROOT OF EVERYTHING

&

LIGHTNING

"Scott Alexander Hess's writing brims with elegant simplicity and pulses with fierce emotional insight."
— Joe Okonkwo, author of *Kiss the Scars on the Back of My Neck* and *Jazz Moon*

"In *The Root of Everything & Lightning*, Scott Alexander Hess uncovers deep affinities between the wide-openness of the American landscape and the wide-eyed optimism of its people—cowmen and farmers, fortune tellers and hard laborers, queer fellows and new women. Sinuously constructed and simmering with eroticism, these short novels nevertheless pack emotional punch. Historical fiction at its cutting-edge best."
—Patrick E. Horrigan, author of *Pennsylvania Station*

"As dense as the Black Forest and as magnificent as an old oak, *The Root of Everything* feels like flipping through a family album of three generations of men, in which Hess has captured brief moments to tell their entire stories of love in all its joy, sorrow and grief."
—Jamie Brickhouse, author of *Dangerous When Wet: A Memoir of Booze, Sex and My Mother*

"*The Root of Everything* takes us from a cold forest in Germany to the complicated promised land of the American Midwest and beyond. This is a story about the forces that shape us—the bonds of blood and love and nature. It's a riveting tale written with both heart and precision."
—Jonathan Corcoran, author of *The Rope Swing*

The Root of Everything

|||||||||||||||||||||||||||||||||||||||||||||| **&** ||||||||||||||||||||||||||||||||||||||||||||||

Lightning

Two Novellas by
Scott Alexander Hess

REBEL SATORI PRESS
NEW ORLEANS

Published in the United States of America and United Kingdom by
Rebel Satori Press
www.rebelsatoripress.com

Paperback ISBN: 978-1-60864-158-1
Ebook ISBN: 978-1-60864-159-8
Library of Congress Control Number: 2021935819

The Root Of Everything

Dedicated to Mary Alice Hess

1

Richard, Germany, 1904

Richard followed his father Wilhelm into the dark canopy of the Black Forest, massive clusters of lean fall trees choking out the dying light of dusk.

They stayed on the perimeter. They were hunting bison. One animal would provide pelts and food for the family through the winter freeze. Richard's younger brother Rolf had stayed behind with their mother Marta. Wilhelm did not like leaving her alone in the cottage for fear of traveling gypsies and bandits. It was the final hunt before the brothers left for America.

The two men moved slowly across earth strewn with dead leaves and Richard thought the hordes of trees looked hungry, like hard black bones soaring to the sky. Hunting was the only time he spent alone with his father. Wilhelm spoke very little as they crept forward. It would soon be night.

They approached a towering oak whose bark was ghostly pale and curling in several spots, as if the tree were losing its skin, dying slowly. Wilhelm stopped, pointing through the trees to a cloud of dust rising in the field just beyond the forest's edge. He hunched down, shouldering his rifle and Richard did the same, though he had no gun. Not far from the perimeter, the strange billowing dust rose like smoke.

"*Schau*," Wilhelm said softly, telling Richard to look more closely.

Richard stared at the swirling earth as it blew. They had come upon two bison.

The animals were preparing for battle, likely over a mate, each falling to the dirt and rolling on its hairy and wide back, fearsome heads rearing skyward, exchanging deep guttural moans. Richard and Wilhelm huddled behind the shield of trees, watching the animals. The two bison first stood far apart, tossing mighty heads and rich dark manes, then slowly walked toward one another grunting. They passed each other, then turned back rushing antler to antler, butting heads.

"*Es ist* für terriotory," Wilhelm said.

As they fought for territory dominance, the field dust stirred and blew more violently. Richard and Wilhelm could not see for these new fast blowing clouds of disturbed earth, but they heard tearing sounds, dark growling cries and powerful grunts. At last there came a long and passionate cry, then quiet.

The dust settled and Richard saw one of the beasts moving slowly away, leaving the victor strutting and stamping his hooves. As the winning bison turned toward them, tossing back its head like a king returning from battle, Wilhelm aimed his shotgun and shot it dead between the eyes. The animal cut loose a dreadful and dark cry as it began to fall, a sound that moved slowly through the night air, echoing longer than it should. The beast was on one knee as if fighting death, defying the hunters, and Richard could not look away. He wanted that dark, mean howling to stop and he wished the animal would fall. The proud bison stayed suspended there, refusing until Wilhelm fired another shot and with one deep bark the thing crumpled, destroyed. They waited, to make sure the other bison did not return.

"*Er ware in schones biest,*" Willhelm said, calling the animal fine.

Richard looked at his father.

"*Vater?*" he said.

Wilhelm was staring at the felled bison and he would not look away nor acknowledge his son. He seemed transfixed. Finally, he got up and went out to the field and Richard followed. With his hunting knife, Richard expertly cut the beast's throat to assure its death and to begin the process of butchering it and preparing the parts to be taken home. They would quarter and strip the beast, claim the fur on its back and the pelt of its body, then make a fire in the woods and camp.

Already the cold night sky was star lit. As Richard cut, Wilhelm spoke softly. At first Richard thought his father was muttering to himself, or reciting something, but soon he realized Wilhelm was speaking to him directly, though in this odd hushed tone.

"*Mein Sohn,*" Wilhelm whispered. "*Warum gehst du mit deinem Bruder nach Amerika?*"

As Richard gently pulled thick, rough skin off beastly shoulder, Richard considered his father's question of why he had agreed, with his brother Rolf, to go to America that winter. He placed his hunting knife in the lower breadth of the beast's back, slicing deeply.

"*Rolf ist ein Träumer,*" Richard said.

Indeed, his younger brother Rolf was a dreamer. He kept Richard up at night, sharing things he learned about

America, stories of outrageous wealth and ingenuity, but mostly about the dazzling St. Louis World's Fair of 1904. Rolf devoured every bit of information he could find about the Fair and became obsessed with the grandness of it all— the introduction of the wireless telephone, a treat called an ice cream cone, the giant Ferris wheel.

His father had made it clear that he did not like the idea of either of his sons leaving Germany, but if they did, they should go together. Richard was the older and smarter of his sons and Wilhelm was certain Rolf would not survive without him. Richard had always looked out for his younger brother.

"*Wir machen euch zum stolzen Vater,*" Richard said, promising his father that his sons would make him proud in America.

His father did not look at him, but lifted his arm and placed it on his son's shoulder for a moment before sighing and turning away.

Once the bison was properly destroyed, they took the pieces into the forest and they made camp, leaving behind only hunks and useless bits, and a wide swath of blood where the beast had so majestically fallen.

2

Cal, Missouri, 1951

It stretched out like farm land, and to Cal and Josie it was mysterious and immense, for it held their future.

An acre, unplowed, untouched, black earth tangled with clumps of dandelions and an empty milk bottle. The late morning sun hitched high, drenching the earth with light, falling over the top of a restless horizon. Cal threw his arm over his wife's shoulder.

Josie was a striking girl in a flowered linen dress. She had a silk pink ribbon tying back her hair, which was thick and richly colored, similar to the dark earth at her feet. It was very hot, even for July in Missouri. Josie was three months pregnant.

"We need a tree," she said. "A big oak to give us some shade."

She laid out a checkered cloth for them to sit. Cal had brought an early lunch. They sat and Cal served cheese sandwiches and Coca Cola. Across the way, looking east past two other such untouched plots of earth, they saw a fence and the golden outline of a mare. Her tail shuddered. Past her, a vegetable garden, then a house.

Their plot was on a hill. There were three more plots already sold, also on the hill. Cal was the first to start building. The hill sloped down to a two-lane road, and past that was a large swath of woods, trees wild and tangling. It was a brand new development that promised to grow into a thriving suburb. Josie had wanted to live in Huntleigh Hills near her family, but Cal said they couldn't afford it.

"Will there be a kitchen window?" Josie said. "Can you put it by the sink so I can look out while I wash the dishes?"

"Your Grandfather Beddenfield all but drew up the blueprints," Cal said.

"Well he is giving us the lumber," Josie said.

Cal bent down and ran his hand through the earth. He held a clump in his palm. He was committed to paying back every cent to her grandfather but he'd only been working at the Beddenfield family lumber mill a year, so he had to save up.

"Sure, we will have a kitchen window," Cal said.

"This seems so far out," Josie said. "I don't think there's a church for five miles."

"It's not Huntleigh Hills but you knew that when you married me," Cal said, brushing the dirt off his hands. "This place will be booming by the time our son is born."

"So you've decided it's a boy?" she said.

"My mother told me," he said.

She turned, startled, and her face went pale.

"Did she?" Josie said softly.

"Yeah, she's pretty good at predicting things," Cal said.

Josie gingerly picked up a sandwich but did not bite into it.

"We had gypsies come to our back door when I was a girl to tell fortunes. My mother wouldn't let us speak to them."

"What did they want?"

"Food or money. But we were poor," Josie said.

"Nobody living in those big houses in Huntleigh Hills is poor, Josie," Cal said.

She set down her sandwich and turned to face him. Her cheeks had regained their rosiness.

"Grandfather Beddenfield built our house and my mother worked every morning at the bakery so we could go to Catholic school. I made my own dresses," she said.

"As if having a new dress is important."

Josie set down her cola, considering the question. Just then, the reddish head of a creature crested up over the hill. It hunched close to the ground, surveying the couple.

"Don't move," Cal said.

It was a small, hungry looking red fox. Cal stood up slowly.

"What does it want?" Josie said.

"Food. Like the gypsies."

Josie reached out to swat him, but Cal was already moving slowly toward the fox with a part of his sandwich.

"Cal," Josie said. "Stay away from it. It might bite you."

Cal moved a few more steps, then tossed the food at the fox. The animal snatched the sandwich and turned away from them, eating. Cal began to move closer.

"Cal!" Josie yelled.

Hearing her cry, the animal fled, leaping down the hill, back across the road and into the stretch of woods.

"Dear God, Cal!" Josie said. "It might have rabies. What else is hiding in those woods?"

He went back and sat by her.

"That all will be cut down within the year. It's all gonna go. This is prime land around here, it's going to be developed,"

Cal said.

"You don't know that," she said curtly. "Did you ask your mother?"

"Can you trust me on this?"

He took her hands.

"I know this isn't where you wanted to settle. But this area is going to boom. It's a good investment, and it's something I can do for us. Something I can make happen for us."

Josie sighed.

"All right," she said.

They finished their lunch then folded up the cloth and headed back to the Chevy. Cal leaned on the steering wheel, which was hot to the touch. The windshield squared off his view to their plot, softening it like a frame in a motion picture.

"This is a good thing, Josie," he said.

Cal trailed his hand across the Chevy's inside windshield, over the landscape as seen through that glass, slowly, as if he could slice into the massive stretch of trees, destroy each last one and reveal beyond the pine, black jack oak and elm their glittering future. Then he brought his hand back onto the steering wheel.

"Flying during the war, I used to dream about this moment," he said. "You and me right here, building a home. Having a son. I didn't know if we'd ever get here."

Josie scooted across the hot seat and ran her fingers over the top of Cal's hand on the wheel.

"Well, I knew we would," she said.

Cal turned to her.

"I want to call him Ricard after my Dad."

Josie frowned.

"No. We will call him Stanford," she said.

"After the man that built the railroad?"

"Yes. And he was a Senator. And started Stanford University. Your mother isn't the only one with superstitions. Just give in on this one Cal, I've got my reasons."

He laughed softly. She bent to him and kissed his cheek.

"Yeah," he said.

She stayed next to him on the seat as he sat up straight, started the car and drove off humming a song he recalled from the war about a place that cooked seafood in a fire pit.

3

Stanford, St. Louis, 1966

They stood at the top of the mighty hill, lean and stiff like stark winter saplings, unwavering in the frigid December midnight. The wind was brutal, the sky clear. At the bottom of the steep incline with its grass beaten and ghostly gray, the lake basin shone still and black.

"I don't have a swimsuit," Bo said.

Stanford considered this. Did the lunk-head actually think they would stand at the edge of the water shivering and put on swimwear? Things had to be timed precisely to avoid hypothermia. It was 28 degrees.

Bo finished his beer, crushed the can in his fist, then paused with deep intention before hoisting it into the air. He and Stanford were both on the swim team, but Bo also wrestled varsity and pitched for the baseball team. The can soared in a fine arc toward a full moon that seemed to be blazing white-hot in the frigid winter sky.

"Just do what I tell you," Stanford said. "And don't lollygag."

Behind them, the St. Louis Art Museum rose and hovered, all stone and stately pillars, the creation of Cass Gilbert who had also designed the Woolworth Building in New York, and who was born on this very night, November 24 of 1859.

The museum was built during the St. Louis World's Fair of 1904 in homage to the Roman baths of Caracalla, which is why Stanford decided they had to swim in its shadow, in a way that was decadent and important, that summoned some phantom sense of another era and honored a human being like Cass Gilbert.

The whole midnight swimming scheme came to him in a dream, and once the idea had settled in, he could not shake it. Stanford's ideas often became obsessions. They had to be done, no matter the consequences. He believed there was a rhythm to fate and he was superstitious, something bred into him by his Granny Emma.

They moved swiftly down the hill, to the edge of the lake basin. There was a concrete lip surrounding the lake, with a step down into the frigid water.

"Get undressed," Stanford said.

He did not move, rather turned to watch Bo. He was blonde, slightly taller than Stanford, and had the highly defined muscularity of a swimmer. He was considered handsome, in a delicate way. Stanford was willowy and had once been called elegant by an elderly aunt on his mother's side, the Beddenfields.

"Hurry up," Stanford said.

Bo was easy to boss. He relied on Stanford's intellect to keep them out of trouble, and his sense of adventure to keep them entertained. They had met as boys at his grandfather's lake house, on Stanford's twelfth birthday, and had been inseparable ever since. Bo tore at his coat, then his clothing. The wind kicked up and a thin icicle-shaped cloud concealed the moon.

"Shit it's freezing, you crazy fuck!" Bo said.

He was naked, all curved athleticism. Stanford paused to study Bo, who stood as attentive as a soldier awaiting a commander's call, stiffly statuesque against the backdrop of the museum, the park's soaring winter trees and the black liquid sky. Stanford undressed, then quickly stepped off of the concrete lip down into the water. He slunk in, like a night creature submerging for the stealthy hunt. He steeled his mind to the sudden shock of the icy water, the rebellion in his body, the panicked urge to turn back. But he knew just how far they could go, how long they could swim. He was in motion, so not instantly numb, though there was an edging sense of terror, of something forbidden and stupid. There was an electrical pain scoring through him but at the same time, a thrilling and determined sense of a god-like ability to demolish any obstacle and follow through on any whim. Bo followed, yelping loudly as he thrashed naked through the terrible water.

"It burns!" Bo hollered.

They swam out a few feet, Bo doing a choppy butterfly stroke and keeping his head aloft. Stanford swam a measured crawl, hearing his friend only in half blasts as he glided forward, tilting his head to the side for regular breaths. They stopped, and treading, Stanford saw the stately museum rising at the top of the hill, and thought of those ancient Roman baths, that brilliant archaic structure that he imagined had stunk of lust and dissolution.

"Go back!" Stanford yelled, reaching out and smacking Bo on the back, keeping his hand there until Bo lifted his body and began battering at the water again, mildly panicked.

Stanford swam expertly, then gripped the concrete lip edge and yanked himself into the piercing winter air. He triumphantly hoisted his lanky form and raced to their pile of clothes, feeling very much like a water-born creature touched by some forbidden past, tainted yet moving into a brilliant future that he knew they would share.

4

Richard, America, 1905

They rode the rails for a long spell, Richard and his younger brother Rolf, looking out with wild fascination through a railroad car door that slid open with a thunderous roar to reveal what they had only dreamed of—America.

They traveled in steerage by sea from Essen, Germany, then snuck onto a North Pacific railroad car in New York, joining a few hobos who drank much and spoke little, which suited Richard and Rolf as they knew only a few words of English.

It was a frigid November so the railroad car door remained shut and the men shook with cold, though a few times Richard cracked it open to get some air, taking in a clear-eyed view of long flat lands piercing a burnt blue horizon. And after dusk, shimmering things under a full moon. Distant towns and night creatures. At times, a million stars.

At other times, if the train crawled to a stop due to some disruption blocking the track, the night appeared dangerous and lonesome to Richard. This new land, men speaking in a language he did not understand, strange cities and customs, left him momentarily wondering if they had made a grave error in leaving their homeland. He pushed his fears aside, though, holding strong to a bright and bold hope.

During their journey, Rolf spoke constantly of the marvelous things they would see at the St. Louis World's Fair. Richard told him to hush; they needed to work hard and save money before they could think about the fair. Richard worried about his younger brother.

They were heading on the train to a lumber camp in Missouri where there was good work cutting timber, if you could stand the cold and hard conditions. They were lean and hungry and young and ready to work. The very air was lit with possibility.

They hopped off the train in Hannibal, Missouri and set off by foot to Brownsville and the lumber camp. The road snaked along the path of the Blackwater River and through long stretches of wilderness. As the day wore on, a biting wind blew, hard clouds the color of coal thickened and hovered and Richard feared they may be lost. Rolf sang as they walked. As evening came, they approached a steep hill and the road narrowed, bordered by the blackest trees Richard had even seen.

They were sturdy elegant things, Richard thought, the color of black pearls. Rolf wanted to stop to look at these dazzling trees, but Richard yelled at him to keep moving. They climbed the hill slowly, and as they went, the wind took on a new and sudden force. There came a high-pitched howling and a light snow. Richard moved faster, calling to his brother behind him, and he heard animal sounds in the wind, mating cries and warnings, and he thought of the dying bison back in Germany, and he thought of his father.

Rolf was lagging, hollering to his brother that they should stop but Richard moved faster, waving Rolf on, pushing up the hill with a new determination and force. As he reached the peak, there came a new darker howl in the wind and the snow became heavy. Standing at the top of the hill, Richard saw below them a wide swath of woods and a light burning from a fire pit. They had arrived at the lumber camp.

5

Cal, St. Louis, 1926

Cal was in the cellar with his father. They were in the far back room, that shadowed place that smelled rooty and medicinal. It was where the bathtub gin was brewed. The product was decent and the price fair so a few local bars were steady customers during prohibition. Cal had never been allowed to enter this room until now. His father had called him down from the kitchen.

"You pick up payment at Keller's tonight," Richard said.

"Yes," Cal said softly.

Cal was overcome with excitement and fear, but he tried to show neither, standing very still. His father had never asked him to do anything so important, had never really bothered with him at all. Every once in a while, he would turn to Cal at dinner, hollering in his native German tongue, banging his knife on the table in frustration as he struggled with a word or phrase in English.

Today was different. His father was asking him to do a job. An important job. He had to make sure he did it perfectly, so he would ask him to do it again.

The back room had no windows and was lit with three mismatched lamps. The floor was dirt, and there was a makeshift work bench. This closeness, this time spent watching his father measure juniper, berries, water, and grain alcohol, was strange and unsettling. This closeness that he'd dreamed about made him feel hot and uncomfortable, like he had a flu. He knew not to disturb his father, who worked methodically, like a chemist, humming a German song Cal had heard him sing a few times on Christmas. The basement door opened and his mother's voice rang down, along with scents of baked bread and a pot roast.

"Dinner is ready, Richard," she said.

"*Danke*, Emma," Richard called back.

Cal admired the way his father thanked his mother every day for the things she did. The cooking, the laundry, even when she snuck up behind Richard's lanky frame to hug him. His father, silent and stern, would smile and say "*Danke*, Emma." Cal hoped he was as nice to his wife when he had one.

"Go," Richard said. "Tell your mother nothing. *Das ist unser geheimnis*. Our secret."

Cal ran upstairs, holding this hot bright secret close to his heart.

As he ate, he realized that what had begun as a normal day had blown up into something extraordinary. He asked to be excused without dessert. He said he was going to meet a buddy to play stick ball. As he was leaving, his mother got up and gave him a hug at the kitchen back door, pressing a blue bird feather into his hand and whispering in his ear.

"Don't lose this. It will protect you," she said.

She shooed him out and he thought, *Well she knows about this too*. It didn't surprise him. His mother was famous up and down Allemania Street for her soothsaying talents. As he mounted his bike he turned back to catch a glimpse of her standing in the doorway, her hand on her hip, shaking her head as if she knew exactly where he was headed.

He rode his bike quickly to Keller's drug store and arrived just after dusk. Keller's was a long, narrow place with a soda counter and a few well stocked merchandise shelves. He saw no women. Men were throwing dice across a small table in the rear. A few fat, dull looking fellas sat at the counter smoking.

The end of the Dempsey fight was on the radio, so Cal lingered and listened after getting the money envelope from Big Red Mike, named for his flaming hair and huge beer gut. Cal was at the far end of the counter, where the register and the radio sat.

"A symbol of every heavyweight king, Dempsey moves fast around the ring."

A man with a wide saggy face turned and smiled at Cal.

"Want a piece of pie kid?"

"Sure?" Cal said.

"Mike give him a piece of the lemon," said the man, as the announcer continued.

"He's up again, Willard gets on his feet. But Dempsey is on him. Fist reigning. And down he goes, down like a wounded animal, his back turned."

Mike set a piece of lemon meringue pie on the white counter. Cal tore into it. The saggy faced man laughed.

"Best lemon pie in town, right kid?" the man said.

"My mom's is the best," Cal said, gobbling.

Cal noticed the man next to him had a big cut on his lower lip. He was grinning and leaning toward him, as if he wanted to steal the pie. Then he turned to the radio as the announcer's voice rose in volume.

"Willard is driven helplessly against the ropes. He wobbles about, there are only a few seconds remaining now, too late for a finishing blow. Willard's teeth are knocked out. He can barely stand. In this most unusual fight an idol has been born!"

The door to the drug store opened and slammed against the wall. Cal was lucky to see the blue steel pistols first. There were four men. Keeping the envelope tight in his grip, he fell to the floor, touching the bird feather in his pocket. The fat men at the counter turned more slowly as the radio pitched a feverish finale to the fight and Big Red Mike yelled one word.

"Wait!"

Cal had never heard a gunshot. It was louder, more ferocious than he imagined. There were too many shots to count, but from his vantage point, he watched Big Red Mike fall behind the counter. Then the man who ordered him the lemon pie toppled off of his stool, landing next to Cal. He crashed onto his belly, chin smashing into the concrete, eyes wide open in fast death. He was close enough that Cal could see the spittle dripping from his twisted, cut lips. What he thought of, as the bullets ripped, was how sticky the floor felt and how he might crawl and hide somehow. He was shivering and his heart was exploding, but he knew he couldn't die like the fat man on the floor. He had to be smart. He pulled out the feather and put it in his mouth.

The bullets stopped. There was only the sound of men,

grabbing half breaths in agony, then footsteps slow and steady across the floor. The front door remained open. A tall, thin man in a suit and broad-rimmed hat put his foot on Cal's back.

"Who are you?" he said.

Cal knew about criminals; he'd read of bootleggers and Al Capone. He'd seen photos of men with their brains spilt. He did not think of his father in these terms. He had not seen photos of dead kids.

"Nobody," Cal said.

The man kept his foot on Cal's back. He seemed to be considering something.

"Aw shit," he said. "Get up."

Cal stood up as the man turned away. He shoved the money envelope into his pants and followed, shot through with fear. He thought his legs might give out but they held. He figured if he tried to run they'd shoot him dead for sure.

"Come on," the man said.

Cal did not look around at the fallen men or the half-eaten pie. He followed the man, out into the summer night, the feather in his mouth, his body trembling with fear, but his legs carrying him forward sure and steady.

6

Stanford, St. Louis, 1967

It was sprawling, stretching for acres, crammed with stripped and knotty beech, maple, walnut, southern pine, ash, black jack oak, all this scenting the mill with something lush, ancient and of the earth. Something sensual and close.

Stanford worked one afternoon a week at the family business, Beddenfield Lumber (his day off from swim practice). When Stanford told his father he wanted to work at the mill to learn about the business before high school ended, his father shrugged, said nothing and put him on the payroll. He was free to set his own schedule.

He was unsupervised and spent his time counting and multiplying the endless rows of timbre, figuring the capacity of the warehouse, the money made, enraptured by the rich wood scents. The lumber triggered in him a strange physical longing, creating sensations that settled inside his mouth, on the nape of his neck, on his palms and feet. In his mind, he wanted to crawl inside of the wood, to nestle into its crevices and its soft insides. At times, he would chew on a stray shard of wood, as a man might chew tobacco. He knew his Grandfather Richard had come to America and worked at a lumber camp in Brownsville, Missouri. He decided timber was in his blood.

Alone in the back warehouse, he got into a habit of standing close to the stacked wood, pressing his cheek against it, imagining the thing's origins, its birth in a far-off wild place, its roots yanked and oozing, its limbs sliced and layers of soft bark mutilated, yet the tree still holding onto its scent, its soul. He knew the value of these cut down trees. Lumber had made his father rich (he married into the business). His mother's family was downright fat with cash from the mill, which was the biggest in Missouri, as well as from a slew of real estate developments all over the city.

His attraction to trees ran deeper, though. His Granny Emma had taken him for walks through the woods when he was a small boy, pointing out roots, flowers and types of bark that would be used in her healing elixirs. She gave the trees human names. She said they all had souls, every growing thing. She said they heard, saw and judged.

He had his eyes shut, cheek on a raw piece of wood and he sensed someone was there, watching. He opened his eyes, almost expecting Granny Emma.

"What are you doing?" said Mr. Buckle.

He was the warehouse manager, a quiet, stocky man just shy of thirty who always wore a suit coat and a wool tie with a fat double Windsor knot. He reminded Stanford of his history teacher.

There was a pause, and Stanford thought he heard Granny Emmy laugh, a delicate trill slipping between the elm and oak. He brushed his shoulder three times to rid the room of bad spirits, a trick she had taught him.

"Nothing," Stanford said.

He took the bit of bark from his mouth, and dropped it to the floor.

"I came to smoke," Mr. Buckle said. "I'm not snooping."

Being the boss's son, few people spoke to or associated with Stanford.

"Have you ever thought of living in the woods?" Stanford said.

Mr. Buckle lit a cigarette, exhaled and considered the question.

"I did live in the woods," Buckle said. "I grew up in Hannibal. It was horrible."

The man spoke freely, which surprised Stanford. Buckle drew on the cigarette, then tugged at his tie. He slouched against a tower of wood. Stanford thought the man acted as if he had nothing to lose.

"I'm moving to New York City," Stanford said.

"Well that's as far from the woods as you can get," Buckle said.

"I didn't say I want to live in the woods," Stanford said.

"No, you didn't."

Mr. Buckle tugged at his tie again, and the fat knot opened wider. Then he unbuttoned the top of his shirt. He had black hair and very pale skin. He was what they called black Irish.

"What does your father think of that?" Mr. Buckle said.

There was a huge set of double doors leading to the front of the mill and when the doors swung, a wind swept through the warehouse. Someone had just pushed the doors open and Mr. Buckle's hair moved with the breeze.

"Mr. Buckle, you back there?" a voice yelled.

"Yes," Mr. Buckle called back.

"You're needed in the front office," the voice yelled.

Mr. Buckle dropped and stubbed his cigarette with his shoe. Then he picked up the butt, and put it in his jacket pocket. He took off his sport coat and slung it over his arm. His white dress shirt was sheer, revealing what Stanford would consider a fighter's physique. Stanford stepped away from the raw wood, stepped toward Buckle with a sensation that he could glide from one hard woodsy scent into a new one, into this man's scent that had begun to build from the moment he stopped there, lit his tobacco, undid his tie, pulled off his coat, and flexed his fighter's arm. Stanford had a strong urge to touch Mr. Buckle, to chew on him like a raw bit of wood. He wanted the man between his teeth.

"Sorry to bother you," Buckle said, turning to go.

Stanford took a few more steps forward, as if to follow Buckle, but stopped, watching him climb the slight hill from the inventory to the huge double doors, watched his shoulders rise and fall, his legs stomp heavily upward, his coat swinging like a paper ax. The light emanating through the double doors swallowed Buckle as he disappeared, but Stanford did not look away for some time.

7

Richard, Brownsville, 1905

There was a log cabin for the foreman, Mr. Herron, and drafty barn-like barracks for the men. There was one cook, a mess hall and miles and miles of towering trees to be slaughtered.

Their first night arriving at the camp, the wind was thick with hard, pebble-sized bits of ice, and the snow beat mercilessly at anything taking a breath.

Richard and Rolf huddled at a huge fire pit near Herron's cabin. A torn up oak tree crackled and hissed, dying in flame. They drank near-frozen beer as Herron told them what he paid, this based on trees cut, not hours spent.

"I'll tell you straight," Mr. Herron said loudly over the wind's roar. "We've lost a few already this winter. Accidents. I need hearty men."

Richard nodded. He only knew a few of the English words. He could see Herron's face lit by the pale and soaring fire, towering licks of flame cutting through the white-iced night.

"Yes," Richard said. "Yes."

Herron was a stout man with a full head of dark black hair and deeply red cheeks. He was covered in a massive quilt-like coat made up of a dozen animal furs: fox, raccoon, coyote. He had one gold tooth in the front of his mouth, which shone like a jewel when he spoke.

Richard and Rolf shared a single bag made of the skin of the bison he'd shot with his father. The bag held one change of clothes each and Rolf's trumpet, which had been passed down to him from his great-grandfather. They wore heavy wool sweaters under their coats and gloves knitted by their mother, as well as sturdy lace-up boots. They had brought nothing else.

"I gotta say you two look sort of desperate from where I sit. You need to be strong for this work," Herron said.

Richard knew the word strong, *kraftig*.

"Yes," he said. "Strong."

Richard sat forward, wanting to speak, to find the words to say *We need work, we need work now. We will work very hard. We don't care what it is. We cannot go back. We are Germans like you Mr. Herron.* But his tongue was heavy and thick and he was tired and through the raging night wind he saw doubt in the big man's eyes.

"I was born here in Missouri but my folks come from Heidelberg," Herron said. "Still, I need to know you can work hard."

Herron looked first at Richard, then at Rolf. Rolf stood up, hoisting his glass of beer and singing, his voice bellowing loudly despite the weather.

"*Ein Prosit, ein Pro sit. Der Gemulichkeit.*"

He held the last note, with deep longing and a rich sadness. It was a drinking song from back home. Richard and Rolf sang it with their father and mother on Christmas and Boxing Day.

Through the flame, Mr. Herron's gold tooth curled against blue lips. And for a moment, Richard felt a hard weight pressing upon him, as if each bit of ice and snow falling was laden with despair, and he felt suddenly how tired he was, how beaten down by the trip and he did not know what they would do if they did not get this job. He saw in the blinding white snow the searing eyes of his father, who had not wanted his sons to leave Germany. Richard looked to Rolf and he could no longer hide his fear, and Rolf looked at him and smiled, then fished into their bag and pulled out his trumpet.

"You play that thing?" Herron said.

Rolf wet his lips and cracked his fingers and despite the biting cold, he began to play. It was the simple but rousing ancient battle song, *Ein Jager Aus Kurpfalz*. As Rolf blew the horn and the notes grew and soared, Richard thought of the cry of the dying bison. Several men wandered up from the camp barracks. One stepped close to Rolf. He was thin as a fishing pole with a shock of white blond hair that shot skyward like a flame. He smiled.

"You bringing them on, Mr. Herron?" the man said. "We could surely use some music."

Herron grunted. Rolf finished the song, as the men stood warming themselves at the fire.

"What else you know," said the thin blond man. Mr. Herron stood up.

"You two can start in the morning," he said, leaving them at the fire.

"My name's Carney," the blond man said. "Welcome to the crew."

He extended his hand, and Richard knew that was good, grabbing and shaking the man's hand with force, as Rolf began to play another song.

8

Cal, Hawaii, 1939

During his first months manning a fighter plane in Hawaii during World War II, Cal felt he was tearing clouds in half, breaking matter in two when he flew. Each time his wildcat fighter moved through a cirrus or cirrocumulus patch, he got a strange sensation of destruction, not related to his real duty, which was to shoot down the Japanese enemy. It was a different feeling all together, a feeling he kept to himself since it scattered his mind in too many directions, and yanked up some dark and ancient grief he couldn't begin to understand.

For a short time he tried to avoid clouds, though that desire had to be shelved. He had a job to do. Lives to save. He flew alone in a one-seater so he could talk to himself to rid these queer ideas. After a while, he did chase them out by painting the face of his foes on the clouds, thus developing a hate for clouds, a new eagerness to slice them to bits.

On the ground, at the shore side bar with the other service men, he never mentioned the clouds. He talked mostly of his girl Josie back home. He also made the mistake of mentioning his job with the Eagan Rats.

"Yeah he's a bona-fide gangster," said Pistol.

Pistol was tall and thin as a pool cue, with big flipper-like hands and feet meant for a gorilla. He was from New Jersey and he and Cal hit it off from the get go. They both had girls back home. They liked the bar because it played American songs on the radio.

Fodo-de-yacka saki want some seafood mama

"Get us some pineapple whiskey Pistol!"

This came from three drunken sailors slouched over a table, singing along with the radio.

Want   some   sea   food,   Mama
Shrimps and rice they're very nice.

"Tell us about the night with the Irish Rats," Pistol said.

He was drinking from a pitcher of beer that he passed to Cal. The place was crawling with all ranks of service men and loose local girls.

"I never did much with the Rats," said Cal. "Cut it out, Pistol."

Pistol called the three sailors over.

"He outsmarted a gangster," said Pistol. "He was a punk, and he made them believe he was Irish."

"I am Irish," Cal said.

"Half German, you told them one hundred percent bona-fide Irish," Pistol said.

"All right, lay off," Cal said.

"He was six years old."

"I was twelve for Pete's sake," Cal said.

The sailors hooted for no reason.

"They plugged ten men in a drug store in St. Louis, blood and guts all over the walls, but our Cal ducked every bullet,"

Pistol said.

Pistol was standing, the three drunk sailors enraptured.

"They took him to a hideaway ready to cut him open, but this one, he thinks fast, says he was on his way to get his Ma some milk," Pistol said.

Cal took a long slug of beer. There was no stopping Pistol once he had an audience.

"I said I was listening to the fight on the radio and yeah sure I told them I was Irish," Cal said.

"See! He outfoxed those fast-talking gangster, then guess what!"

"They shot him!" one of the sailors, the one with white blonde hair and steely biceps said. "Now get us that Pineapple whiskey, Pistol!"

"No, he got a job. Running deliveries. They bought his wide-eyed story and that's that. He's a gangster now!"

Pistol took a bow, as if he'd performed a bit of Shakespeare and the three sailors applauded loudly.

"I'm done with all that," Cal said.

"Here we go," said Pistol. "Love!"

"Yeah, yeah," Cal said.

Across the bar, a girl with the hair the color of licorice and skin like cocoa with milk smiled at him. His friend was right. He was in love. He promised his girl Josie he'd stop doing jobs for the Rats. She wanted him to go into her family's lumber business. She whispered that in his ear, tugging on the back of his head, twining her fingers in his hair and asking him if he would. If he survived this war, he figured that was what he'd do.

Pistol sat down, eyeing up the crowd.

"That tiny one in the corner wants you bad," Pistol said.

"I hear she's a tiger."

"I'd rather go swimming," Cal said.

"Yeah?" Pistol said.

The girl was moving to their table, but the white-blonde sailor stopped and gripped her hard around the waist.

"I got a motorcycle. You want to drive somewhere?" Pistol said.

"I said I want to go swimming. It's hot," Cal said.

"You just want to get out of buying a round. Get those wet dopes some whiskey."

Cal got up and went to the long crowded bar. The radio droned on, tugging at him, American songs scratchy and out of whack way over here. Everything was out of tune over here.

The only thing he liked these days was flying planes. His mind scattered on a steel blue horizon, that sense of life dropped off all around, nothing mattered much, until a target appeared. Truth was he'd seen very little action.

He couldn't wait to get back home. To see Josie, and his folks. He checked his pocket for the frayed blue feather. It was there. He carried that, along with a hollow blue bird's egg his mother had given him. He'd never tell Pistol, but he was pretty sure these Irish charms kept him from harm's way, even over here, even up a thousand feet in the air.

"Take the bottle," said the barkeep, passing over the pineapple whiskey.

Cal took it and headed back to his table, pretty sure he could convince Pistol to go for a midnight swim.

9

Richard, Brownsville, 1905

The sky had gone a soft grey at dusk, promising snow and casting the woodlands in a gentle hush. The evening wind was high-pitched and increasingly strong. It would dip below zero soon. The men were happy to end their day. Some were getting to town, others had bottles and would gather, sharing stories in the barracks. It was Christmas Eve.

Richard and Rolf huddled near the pit fire. They had agreed to work late for extra pay.

"Get on" yelled Carney. "It's Christmas ye' greedy fucks."

The brothers had saved nearly enough money for a two-day trip to the St. Louis World's Fair before it ended. This extra work would cinch it. Rolf was overjoyed.

Carney ambled toward the fire. He was well liked, as was Rolf. Richard did not join the men in card games or drinking songs and did not linger talking after hours. He was respected, but not liked. Richard also was not as adept at picking up English.

"Hey," Rolf said.

Carney offered Rolf a slug from a bottle nestled under his coat. Richard lifted a hand in protest, catching his younger brother's eye. They had to tackle the demon tree before nightfall, the one mighty cedar that hadn't been cut down that day as was planned. Mr. Herron hated to be off schedule.

"Merry Christmas," Carney said, slapping Richard on the back. "You both come to my bunk when you're done destroying that tree. You can tell me all about what you lugs did on Christmas back in Germany, and what you're gonna see first once you get to the fair. See ya later, Rolf."

The men sang as they drifted into darkness, away from the fire's light. Richard looked up at the sky as it started to snow. It did not begin slowly, rather rushed forth with a mighty burst, like a thread had snapped on a high up casing releasing thousands of snowflakes. The wind sang high and hard. He thought of last Christmas back home, eating his mother's Christmas Strudel. Through the increasing wall of snow came Mr. Herron.

"You still think you can do this?" he said.

Drawing closer to the fire, his black hair dusted white with snow, he yelled in German to them.

"*Kannst du in diesem sturm arbeiten?*"

"Yes," Richard said.

Richard slapped Rolf on the shoulder and drew him away before Mr. Herron changed his mind. They moved toward the eight-foot two-man saw and the demon tree. Richard had great faith in their combined strength and the grace of Christmas. He was sure they could get through this tree before the pitch-black hit or the snow started to pile too high and drift. The snow was turning in on itself, blowing in a chaotic dance, wild and untamed with a newly fearsome wind. He motioned to his brother.

The earlier sound of men singing was completely blighted by the wind, the hollering had stopped and the only light was the one burning in the cabin where Herron lived. They reached the tree as the first bits of hail smacked their cheeks. Richard yelled to Rolf and they started.

They each gripped their side of the long powerful saw and set into the oak end to end. They could barely see one another through the heavy mast of growing storm, but the saw's teeth clenched, their arms straining, those long jaws of metal biting into the tree, moving slowly and surely.

"*Stetig*," Richard yelled, reminding Rolf to keep it steady and smooth.

They found a rhythm, the dance in twos, a movement which would continue with gentle force, moving through the beastly thing, severing its life, pulsing into it bit by bit.

There was in the howling wind the high cry of a powerful winged creature, a crested flycatcher Richard thought as he moved in time with his brother. The hail picked up, pelting his head, tapping his frozen cheeks, but he kept on.

He looked across at Rolf just for a moment, but in that moment the teeth caught a snag, some uneven tear in the inner guts of the tree, a reckless twist. As the saw connected and was jolted by the flaw, the thing snapped out of their hands, yanking out of the innards of the tree and vibrating forth into the gray and icy wilderness. Richard was thrown back, and he thought *that is the hand of God*. But as he stood up, as the hail increased, slashing at him, he saw his brother in a heap, where the wild and shaking saw had left him, cut nearly in half.

10

Cal, St. Louis, 1942

Josie's house was in Kirkwood, on a street where the trees bloomed in spring with pale pink flowers and neighbor ladies wore a dress and hat just to cross the yard and say hello. It was a sturdy, two-story house, painted white and built with wood from Josie's grandfather's lumber yard. It had a grand front porch and a grander front lawn.

The cement houses on Allemania where Cal lived didn't have porches, let alone lawns. Allemania had a common narrow street where kids played and people gathered in summer. It all looked toward St. Bridgit's cemetery with its towering, ancient trees and forgotten graves.

Cal stood looking at Josie's house. He wore his Air Force uniform. His shoes were shined. There was a light shining in the second-floor window. That was Josie's father's room, Mr. John Fitzgerald. He was bed-ridden, mustard gas from the first war manifesting in lung disease.

Cal had a bouquet of daisies for Josie. It was a warm evening and he was afraid he would sweat through his undershirt straight to his starched uniform.

He made his way across the looming front lawn, toward the porch, toward the front door, toward her father. The door swung with a bang and a white-haired teenager stepped to the lip of the porch, hovering on the steps that led up. It was Josie's brother Bill.

"Where'd you get the flowers, the graveyard?" Bill said.

Bill was tall and lean and Josie said he loved to make trouble. He blocked the way onto the porch.

"Hey Bill," Cal said.

From behind the screened front door, Josie spoke.

"Go on, Bill," she said.

Bill took a boxer's pose and threw a few fake punches, then ran past Cal out into the yard. The door swung again and Cal went in. Josie took the flowers, then sent him straight up the stairs.

"He's waiting for you," she said.

He left her at the foot of the curling stairway that led to the second floor. Framed needlework hung on the walls. At the threshold, he turned toward the light, the large bedroom at the end of the hall where Josie's father was laid up. He went to the door, then hesitated.

"Come on," said Mr. Fitzgerald.

Cal walked in. The room was bigger and brighter then he'd imagined. Josie's father was sitting up in a four-poster bed which faced the two front windows, both open wide to the evening. He was a large man, over six feet, with a thick head of tar black hair. His feet reached the end of the bed and he wore striped pajamas. He was very, very pale but he did not look that ill.

His bed was covered with books, and on his bedside table were more books. In addition to the overhead light, there were four bold lamps on tables, and this intense and unexpected brightness made Cal recall those hot war days, the islands, that noon sun blazing by the water where loose girls splashed around and taunted the soldiers with promises.

"So you want to marry my daughter?" Mr. Fitzgerald said.

Then the man began to cough. It began slowly, like a growl, then it escalated, a gradual rise of force and intensity erupting into a raucous loud hacking as if he would heave up his insides.

"John!"

A woman's voice from downstairs. Cal moved a few steps toward the bed, mildly panicked. There were three more long howling hacks, then Mr. Fitzgerald spit into a blood smeared handkerchief, gasping.

"Get me a drink," he said. "Whiskey on the table. Hurry up."

Cal fetched it. Mr. Fitzgerald gulped it and signaled for another.

"Get yourself one, these are heady topics," he said.

There was a chair next to the bed. It was rough-hewn, pine Cal guessed, hand stained, the back spindles wrapped together with thick twine. He sat gingerly.

"You can't break that, Mae's father made that at the Beddenfield mill, it's a relic but sturdy as they come."

Mr. Fitzgerald was red in the face from coughing. He took three long deep breaths. He slumped and Cal thought it was as if since he walked in, since the coughing fit, the night was draining the life out of the man.

"I know what you want," Mr. Fitzgerald said. "So, we better get to the meat of all of this."

"John!"

The woman's voice again.

"Holler down we are fine," Mr. Fitzgerald said.

Call yelled.

"All right, but send that boy back down here soon," the voice said.

"My wife Mae, you don't want to mess with her, so this is what I have to say."

From below, a clock chimed eight times. From outside, a voice yelled. Cal wondered if it was Bill.

"If you marry my daughter, and I imagine you will as she is as stubborn as her mother and for whatever godly reason her mother approves of you, I'd like you to go into the lumber business. I'd like you to take up what Mae's father so freely offers. He has no son, only a daughter Mae, and he had his hopes set on my taking over the Beddenfield mill. Now my sons, well, I don't have time to go into that, but they having highfalutin ideas of what they intend to do with their lives and it does not include lumber. So that is what I would like you to do."

The speech wore the man down. His face was flushed.

"I would be grateful if you went into the business," Mr. Fitzgerald said.

He slumped, sunk lower into the bed, shut his eyes.

This was not what Cal expected. Courting Josie, he had only heard how much her father did not approve of him or of where he came from (bootleggers and bums live on Allemania Street), and what he might do with his life (he ran with the Eagan Rats).

"So?" Mr. Fitzgerald said, eyes still shut.

Cal had thought of working his way up with the Rats, thought of learning carpentry like his father, or being a pilot and flying planes, but high over all of that, high and sweet calling and tugging at the back of his hair like she did, there was Josie. And then, staring at Mr. Fitzgerald slumping (*dying,* he thought, *what if he's dying?*) Cal saw more fully this room, the immensity of it, the stark shining lights, oil paintings on the walls, the crystal decanter where the whiskey smoldered and even the drapes, finery, things never imagined on Allemania Street with its burlap window coverings and teetering kitchen tables and rot. This was Josie's world. She had needs. Her all pink and rosy as the flowering trees out front, past her teasing brother and houses even grander than this one with tennis courts in their back yards. She was, after all, part Beddenfield from her mother's side, and that family was quite something.

"Yes sir," Cal said. "I'd be happy to work at the lumber mill."

Mr. Fitzgerald slowly opened his eyes, looked slightly befuddled, then regained his focus and forced himself up, speaking slowly and clearly.

"You will not work there," he said. "You will run the place someday, young man."

11

Rolf's Retreat was perched high on a hill overlooking the decaying town of Brownsville. At dawn, fog hovered thickly, swathing the retreat's house and grounds, creating a netherworld of misty darkness punctuated by distant animal cries and rattling winds.

Stanford was spending his twelfth birthday there. It was his grandparents' country place, named after Stanford's long dead Uncle Rolf. Sleeping on a cot in a small room, which was empty save for a few yellowed drawings of monstrous looking trees stuck up on the wall, Stanford woke. He could see nothing out of the window by his bed. The fog had surrounded the house and dreamily he wondered if the whole place had been pulled up into the clouds.

"Do you think there's something hiding in that mist?"

The voice was high pitched, like a child's, mischievous but gentle. It was his Granny Emma, in the doorway, barefoot in a stark white dressing gown, her snow-white hair twined in a peak atop her head as if she had been borne of the frothy clouds. She was just under five feet tall, bone thin, pale and doll-like, freckles covering her face and arms. Stanford wondered if he should move, or if she might turn and disappear into the walls. She frightened him.

"The men are out for a swim," she said.

"Why didn't they wake me up?" Stanford said.

"You and I are going to make your birthday cake. Come on," she said, turning quickly and disappearing.

From beyond, he heard, "Come to the summer kitchen. Hurry!"

He dressed quickly and made his way out of the house, angry that his father hadn't included him in the morning swim. He thought as he grew older his father might take more of an interest in him, but so far that had not happened. The only thing his father really seemed to care about was running the family lumber mill. Stanford figured someday he'd get a job there, just to see what all the fuss was about.

Rolf's Retreat sprawled across a good ten acres, and consisted of a two-bedroom ranch house, a summer kitchen and a large pond for swimming and fishing. There was also a stretch of flat land filled with huge blackened tree trunks, slaughtered relics of the 1920s lumber boom. The home and summer kitchen were made of knotty pines, sawed and thrust together, left raw and unvarnished. Everything smelled rooty and of wet wood, which Stanford liked.

The sun was high and fine. He saw Granny Emma, still barefoot, white hair flying, as she disappeared into the summer kitchen behind the house. He imagined she brewed potions there at night while he slept. If he woke to the sound of an animal cry, he thought it might be his Granny plucking a furry thing from the woods, snapping its growling jaw and using its thick blood in witchery. On his birthday last year, she'd given him a frayed and yellowed book about Irish fairies, and a speckled blue egg that she said was hollow and should be kept in a drawer to shield him from passing banshees.

The summer house was a big stodgy square, its walls screened for ventilation. In July, temperatures crept past 100. Inside, there was a long wooden table, a few stray and rickety chairs, but the dominant thing was a monstrous oven. It was a relic on claw feet, with four black cooking burners and a wide door that squealed every time it was drawn open. To one side was a shelf for cooling pies and cakes. There was also a baker's rack filled with flour, sugar, spices and unmarked jars, these which Stanford had decided contained potions and animal parts.

She was peeling plums at the table, her fingers stained a deep purple, as if bruised. There were several bowls and a loaf pan plus a pound of butter melting in the morning heat.

"Fetch the flower tin, Stanford," she said.

He brought it then sat beside her as she expertly skinned the fruit.

"Take out the plum pit, the heart of it, then squash it with your hands so it's soft and pulpy," she said. "Put them in that bowl."

She pressed a plum into his palm, her hands nearly as small as his. He dug in a finger and yanked at the pit, then squeezed the fruit tight in his grip, pulverizing it, flooded at once with an odd, uneasy satisfaction. He liked the powerful feeling of flattening the fruit to pulp in his hand.

"This is the cake that cast a spell over your Grandfather Richard," she said, handing over the rest of the skinned plums.

She got a sugar tin and a large mixing bowl from the baker's rack, then set into making the batter, kneading the melting butter into the dry ingredients.

"Tell me the story again of how you met Grandpa," Stanford said.

Granny Emma was crazy, but she told great stories. She looked up from the mixing bowl and smiled.

"Your grandfather was strong and tall, digging deep into the earth the spring we met. I spied on him for a while at first," she said. "My daddy's house was at the end of Allemania Street, facing the cemetery of St. Bridgit's."

Stanford knew that his grandfather had worked as a grave digger, before getting a job as a carpenter.

"He was looking to bring together the two halves of his poor dead brother Rolf," she said, crossing herself. "He didn't know it, but that was it. I knew he was fighting grief, the way he tore into that dirt. So one day I left him a plum cake on a grave stone. Then I watched to see what he would do."

Stanford handed her the crushed plums. She ran her hands through the mash, gently testing it for consistency.

"What did he do then?" Stanford said softly.

"He ate it. And there was no turning back for us after that," she said. "Butter that loaf pan."

They finished making the cake, then she brewed coffee. Stanford didn't tell her he had never drunk coffee. He was twelve now and it seemed like a good thing to do. He wanted his father to see him drinking coffee when he came back. He sipped the muddy liquid gingerly, trying not to grimace. Granny Emma drank hers quickly.

"Shall we tell your fortune, since it's your birthday," she said.

Her hands, which gripped the china mug, were still dark purple. As she stared at him, he was overcome with a strange but comforting feeling, as if they were slipping into a quiet, gentle place where no one could find them. She leaned forward and smiled, then she stared into her cup.

"Oh," she said. "Oh my!"

He leaned in toward her to see, but she pulled the mug back.

"You have a deep secret," she said. "It is barely known even to you. It will bring you great gifts but if you are not careful it could bring you great sorrow as well."

Stanford wondered if she sensed his fear of her, his wonder. She tilted the cup up, dipped her finger in the grounds that lingered at the bottom. She rubbed her ring fingers together then brought them to her lips, her mouth tiny and piqued like a doll. The purple stain from crushing the plums was darker and ruby colored, mixed with the coffee grinds, and Stanford thought it looked like exotic blood. She rubbed the grinds on her lips and shut her eyes. All was still, and it was as if she had forgotten he was there, taking in a breath and saying something so softly he could not hear it. Then she opened her eyes wide and grabbed him by the shoulders, pulling him so close to her that he could smell her, all those sweet and earthy kitchen scents. And he was again afraid of her.

"Did your father give you a gun?" she said, her words fast and ragged.

"No," Stanford said. "He never gave me anything."

His mother bought the presents.

She pulled him even closer with a strange and frightening roughness he did not understand.

"You must never hunt, do you hear me," she said. "There is a beast with shining eyes in the dark and you think you are killing it but it is killing you. Promise me!'

From a distance came the sound of his father and grandfather, singing a German folk song as they approached. He was trembling, as was she. Her eyes grew even wider as if they would turn into a great doorway that would suck him inside of her.

"Promise!" she said.

"Yes, yes," Stanford said. "I promise."

With this, and as the voices grew louder, she loosened her grip and pressed her grind covered fingers gently to his cheeks.

"This is our secret," she said. "Here come the men."

She went to the oven, and Stanford turned to the door as his father and grandfather came in, still wet from swimming, lean and tanned, laughing, diminishing all traces of anything magical.

"The lake is cool today Stan, go for a swim," his father said.

As the men sat down, talking loudly, Granny Emma whirled around.

"Yes, you best go have a swim," she said. "You best go now while the cake cooks. Go on!"

She again had that wild-eyed look. Stanford ran for the door, glad to be out of her sight.

Stanford was barefoot, his fingers stained purple from the squashed plums. He trudged angrily up the hill from the summer kitchen to the lake. He was happy to go for a swim, but the crazed look Granny Emma had given him and the way she ordered him out didn't sit right. Plus, he was still mad that he hadn't been asked to swim with his father and grandfather earlier. He'd been left sleeping like a child. And Granny Emma had rushed him out so fast, nobody had noticed he was drinking coffee.

He stopped and took off his shirt, then hesitated, looked around and quickly took off his shorts and underpants. It was an act of defiance, something clearly forbidden, this offering of his nakedness to the blazing sun, the nearby empty woods, and soon, the soft green lake. He was tanned and tall for twelve, and as he reached the peak of the hill, he raised his arms triumphantly over his head, tilting his face to the sky, howling in the voice of an imagined tribal warrior. There were no birds above, but he heard a cawing. Lowering his gaze, he saw a boy, flailing not too far out in the water, a tow-headed figure. For a moment, he shuddered with a clear and burning knowledge, clarity of knowing that Granny Emma had sent him for a reason.

He ran at a clip and threw himself naked into the lake all while hearing his own echoing howl, seeing the face of that just imagined warrior, feeling a rush of burgeoning masculinity and strength as he thrashed toward the flailing boy, cutting through the emerald water and slicing into a thin thread of blood. He was a strong, graceful swimmer and made it to the kid easily, his heart pounding, his mind racing with the knowledge that he was very important in this moment of saving. He wished his father could see him.

Once he got to the kid, he spoke to him in a quiet and reasonable voice, told him to stay still, recalling his life saving class at school. Things slowed down. He got behind the boy, thrusting his left arm over the kid's left shoulder, across his chest, catching his fingers under the boy's armpit. Then he began to swim an easy back stroke using his right arm and both legs to propel them toward shore.

The boy was breathing more easily, letting him take control, and the two moved as one. Stanford enjoyed the extreme closeness, skin on skin, the boy's tangled hair near his chin. His hand cupped the boy's armpit, which was soft with strands of hair. Stanford swam at a slow pace enjoying the sensation of his legs kicking then coming together gently, pressing close to the boy he was saving. He recalled bold images he'd seen of the Greek God Poseidon. He'd secretly torn a page out of one library book which showed Poseidon bare chested, mighty head thrown back, eyes wide in victory over the sea. The boy did not seem to notice or care about their pace. Stanford figured he was glad to have a great swimmer like him to save his life.

When they reached the shore, Stanford laid the kid on the grass, then stood behind him so he could catch his breath and spit water. He bent down and pressed the boy's blonde hair away from the gash, to get a closer look at it.

"It's not so bad," Stanford said. "I had a cut on my leg that bled a lot more than that."

The blond boy sat up slowly.

"Thanks," he said, touching the cut on his forehead. "I dove under out there and hit my head. I got scared."

The boy turned around looking at him, and as he did Stanford's breath slowed, as did his mind, and with that slowing Stanford began to settle back into his actual life. He sat down to diminish his nakedness, pulling his knees to his chest. The grass was itchy on his ass. He looked around, forgetting where exactly he had dropped his shorts.

"I'm Stanford. Our house is just over the hill."

"Bo," the blond boy said. "Our place is down the road, past the woods. Is this your lake?"

"Yeah, but you can swim here anytime. But I best teach you a few things first. I'm a champion swimmer," Stanford said. "I've got three medals for the crawl stroke and I passed my life saving course."

Bo smiled broadly.

"Yeah? I swim at school too. My specialty is the butterfly."

"Well what happened to you out there then?" Stanford said.

Bo laughed, rubbed his hand over his face, and lay back on the grass.

"Don't tell anybody," Bo said.

Stanford lay next to him.

"Ok. But you owe me one."

They stayed there for a spell, before Stanford lazily retrieved his pants, and invited his new friend Bo up to the summer kitchen for plum cake.

12

Richard, Brownsville, 1905

They put the two parts of Rolf in a burlap bag and buried him under the demon tree that slayed him. The frozen earth was nearly impenetrable, and though the men were not fond of Richard, they liked Rolf, so they hacked, stabbed and shovel-dug the stubborn black earth for hours in the brutal cold to get the toughest layers to surrender. After that icy tangling, they let Richard dig the grave alone.

Mr. Herron gave Richard the pay he owed both he and Rolf and told him of a delivery truck that stopped in nearby Brownsville on its way to St. Louis. He did not try to convince Richard to stay. Men did not want reminders of death.

The road from the camp to Brownsville was long and flat, bordered on both sides by swaths of forest, mighty trees shivering and bucking against a whistling wind, casting a further blackness over Richard's already bleak mood. He carried his bison skin bag with his clothes and Rolf's trumpet. He had considered burying the instrument, but decided he would pass it on to his son, if he had one someday.

He felt the trees swaying with their own angry breath, tossing their fat and naked limbs to and fro, haunting him and threatening to bend down and deliver a fatal blow.

And he heard too, in the wind, the gentle voice of Rolf

singing the German folk songs his younger brother was so
fond of. He stopped often, first to listen, then to search the
empty road for Rolf's spirit, and finally to rage and wail
into the openness, a thick, random grief emerging in searing
and furious bits, shaking his entire body, emptying him of
all energy so he had to sit on the roadside. At one point he
began to claw at the earth, madly and without reason, as if
the digging would uncover some hidden thing, some buried
answer to his grief. He knew he had to write his father about
the tragedy, and this tore at him.

He walked all day. Richard was grateful for the long,
lonesome journey, the terrible cold, the stark endless road,
for he could not stand to stay still. His brother's death did
not diminish his desire to make his way in America; rather,
it turned a soft burning flame into a god-like and histrionic
blaze. He would find his way in St. Louis, though he would
not go to the fair. That belonged to Rolf.

Brownsville was a listless but friendly town that came alive
at night. It was halfway between the lumber camp and St.
Louis, and had sprung up as nothing more than a stopping
point for travelers. There was a trading post and a saloon,
reminiscent of wild nuggets of humanity that flourished
during the gold rush. Richard bought a can of sardines at
the town store, then found the man with the truck who was
traveling to St. Louis. It was a Mack Brother's vehicle chock
full of bags of grain in its back flatbed. The front seat was

over the engine and there was no covering. The wind ripped at them as they drove. The driver's name was Billie Rae, a young man with a crewcut and a bright smile.

"Grateful for the company," said Billie. "Gonna be a cold one."

They drove through the day and talked little at first, due to the loud howl of the wind. By late afternoon the weather had calmed, and Billie struck up a conversation.

"What's waiting for you in St. Louis? A gal?" Billie said. "Are you going to the fair?"

Richard stayed silent. His mind was still caught in the dark tangle of grief, and he understood little English. Rolf had done the talking.

"Ain't much for conversing?" Billie said.

Richard was aware the man was looking at him intently.

"German," Richard said. "No English."

"Oh."

They rode in silence. Richard opened his tin of sardines and offered some to Billie. Billie noticed that Richard's hands were black with dirt, but he said nothing.

"Obliged," said Billie, taking two, then licking his oily fingers as he drove. "You been to St. Louis before?"

"I need work," Richard said.

"Don't know of any, unless you want to dig graves."

Richard knew the phrase. The men at the camp had repeated it to him as they dug Rolf's burial place.

"Yes," Richard said.

"Yes what?" Billie said.

They turned a bend, facing a very long stretch of flat road, bordered on one side by acres of winter gray crops and a two-story farmhouse in the distance.

"Yes you dig graves?" Billie said.

"Yes," Richard said.

The front door of the clean white farm house opened and a woman wearing a blue dress stepped out holding something in her arms. She was not wearing a coat. They passed the house but the image of the woman lingered in Richard's mind.

"Well, they got work at the cemetery at the end of Allemania. There's not a man I know willing to dig winter graves. Pays shit. But if you really need work. I can introduce you to Mr. Remlond. He sets that up."

"Yes," Richard said.

As they drove, he thought several times of the woman in the blue dress and her bundle. He imagined she was holding a child, a boy to be sacrificed to some brutal god of nature. They rode on and Richard shunned his wild thoughts, rubbing his dirt smeared hands together for warmth. He did not turn to look out at the road again.

13

Cal, Steeleville, 1950

"Well that's that."

Cal was lying in the Cedar Lodge motel's twin bed, eyes shut, deeply satisfied, barely dreaming of a stretch of South Pacific sky, when he heard Josie whisper.

"Well that's that."

The room was dark, but he could see her leaning into an oval mirror perched on the top of a blonde-pine dresser. She was naked, her hair a mess, her shape dazzling, so many spots which had been a mystery to him a day ago now revealed. A tiny scar on her stomach, a mole on her upper thigh, the most perfect curve from waist to hip. After they had made love, he had dozed, imagining she lay beside him. Yet here she was, muttering.

The room, which faced a dirt hill leading to Cedar Lake, had thin cotton drapes covered with images of deer and frail looking trees. The sun would be up soon and things would brighten. He rustled the sheet and shut his eyes, feigning sleep. He heard Josie move into the bathroom. She turned on the water.

He got up and dressed, then stopped at the mirror over the dresser. He looked closely, as if the glass held some remnant of her thoughts, that strange phrase. "Well that's that." Not what he expected to hear from his new bride. The words were odd and foreign to him and he could not begin to decipher their meaning, their feminine mystery. Maybe that's what married life was about, mystery.

Light rose through the cheap drapes and he saw in the mirror's reflection their wedding bed, sheets twisted, one pillow cast to the floor. They had gone slowly, and he had tried not to let on how nervous he actually was. They'd had many close moments during their courtship, but making love was something else. In the dark the night before, so close to her, he had felt like he was underwater holding his breath, a little panicked, aware of every touch and movement, excited yet unsure. She had moved against him cautiously, gently, and he felt she was in her own type of dream world. Afterwards, he had fallen asleep quickly.

He stepped away from the mirror and smiled, then went out to get them coffee at the Lodge's diner. He'd have it waiting when she came out.

Their room was at the end of a line of ten, and had two small lawn chairs facing the dirt parking lot, which led straight to the lake. He got back with the coffee and two sweet rolls and set them down near the chairs. The door opened and Josie peered out, wearing a flimsy silk robe covered with pink ribbons.

"Breakfast!" he said.

Cal held his arms over his head in triumph. She smiled.

"You want to eat out there?" she said.

"Sure, nobody's up yet. And we can see the lake," he said.

Josie hesitated, then stepped out, gave him a kiss on the cheek, and sat. Cal served her the roll.

"Well ok," she said.

Cal was struck by the softness of her tone, an odd resignation, the same tone he'd heard just before.

"It's funny," he said, biting into his roll.

"What?"

"I thought..." he began.

He hesitated. What was it he meant to say?

"I thought I heard you say that, something like that," he said.

"What are you talking about, Cal?"

"This morning, you got up before me, I thought I heard you talking."

Josie turned to him, sweet roll mid-air. She still had on lipstick and her eyes were made up. They'd left the wedding and came straight to the Lodge, which was an hour out of St. Louis. She looked at him and took a breath, and kept looking at him and he wished he hadn't said anything, wished she would look away now. It was not a big deal. He didn't want to start off this way. He recalled how his father would so often lift up his mother, say thank you for tiny things, hoist her in the air and make her laugh. He always thought he would do that to his wife but for the moment, he just stared.

"You heard me?" she said. "Well I feel a little strange. Not quite like myself. What did I say?"

Her voice was soft, that same whispery tone. He laughed awkwardly and she looked away.

"Oh I don't know, forget it," he said.

He laughed loudly and took a huge bite out of his roll, making a production of finishing it up and licking his fingers. A few minutes passed, and there was only the sound of the lake down the hill, lapping methodically at a pebble shore.

"What is there to do here?" she said.

Cedar Lodge was nestled in a patch of woods near the tiny town of Steeleville. There was an apple orchard not too far off, but mostly just the big lake for swimming or fishing.

"It's a nice day for a swim," he said. "And I bet we can find a restaurant tonight somewhere."

She nodded and they both looked out at the distant lake, whose water had taken on a clear, white-ish tone as the sun shone brightly.

A black car pulled up and parked three cabins down. A young woman got out, sat on the hood of the car and lit a cigarette. She stared at them with a confidence Cal considered strange for a woman. A very tall, striking man in a suit got out and stretched, waved to Cal and Josie, then went down to the lodge office.

14

Stanford, St. Louis, 1968

They were surrounded by the things they destroyed.

Stanford watched the treetops shake with the hot summer wind, as if heaving their own ancient breath. He decided if they could yank roots and move, they would crush him with their mighty limbs.

He and Mr. Buckle were lying on a blanket under a formidable oak, shaded against the sun at high noon. They had driven an hour out of the city toward Brownsville near his grandparents' summer house. They had parked and walked deep into the forest, Mr. Buckle fussing and fretting until they finally settled under a web of shielding trees. Mr. Buckle was terrified of being found out.

By the time they'd laid down the blanket, and Stanford had stripped, Mr. Buckle forgot his fears, his frail misgivings, and they made love with ferocity.

Now they rested, spent, in the quiet interval which Stanford liked very much. Mr. Buckle was always happy to listen to him talk at length after sex. His other lover, Bo, had no tolerance for that. Bo liked to play loud music and eat after fucking.

Stanford was going away to New York City to attend college in the fall, and he would truly miss Mr. Buckle. Bo was going to the same school, so he'd get plenty of sex, just not much talking.

"I think my mother left us," Stanford said.

They were naked and sweaty, lying side by side. He had never said the words aloud (*she left us, will leave us*), though for years he'd believe in his heart that it would happen. As much as he would miss his mother, he was in awe of her courage and tenacity, her strong desire to carve out what might be left of her life after doing time as a Missouri housewife.

Stanford dug his left hand into the dirt, which was damp from a violent rain storm the night before. The mud seeped between his fingers, a comforting sensation. Mr. Buckle said nothing. Stanford knew he could take his time with the story, that Mr. Buckle would lie quietly and remain attentive. Then they would make love again. The hot sun burnt through a high shield of leaves, settling on their naked feet.

"She's gone to Paris to write and paint. I don't think she will come back this time," he said. "My father says she will, but I think she was waiting for me to go away to school. She's always had a lot of her own money, family money. I think she's going to start to use it.'

Mr. Buckle sighed and Stanford considered what other details to share. All those trips she took, the time she disappeared on his birthday. He sunk his fingers deeper into the mud, then scooped up a handful and rubbed it on his belly. He liked its coolness.

Her leaving hadn't surprised him. The past several years, as Stanford's father spent longer and longer hours at the mill, rescuing it from a downturn then vaulting it to new financial heights, his mother's behavior had become increasingly erratic, whispered about at the mill and the country club. As her husband fell into a money-driven obsession, she moved from the woman she had always been into something Stanford imagined she had at one point dreamed of being. It was as if she had stepped quietly into a soft cocoon of discovery, without regret or complaint, settling into her own season of deep change. He had always understood her, because he felt a lot like her. He had also bided his time in Missouri, with the confidence that he would get to New York City where his real life would begin.

Stanford did not believe his father ever cheated on her or did anything awful, but he seemed to have forgotten her, like a misplaced favorite sweater left too long in the back of the closet. By the time his father realized his fatal error, that he would need to fight hard to keep her, his mother was already too far gone.

"My father is devastated," Stanford said. "He sits on the porch at night and cries. I don't know what to do with him. He seems clueless."

The sun was creeping up their legs, like water rising. Stanford turned to Mr. Buckle.

"What should I do?"

Mr. Buckle looked befuddled. Stanford reached out and caressed the man's inner thigh, for as much as he wanted to solve the sad riddle of his father and that loss, he equally did not want to face it, and would rather dissolve into the mystical rush of sex. Mr. Buckle turned his head. He had a very broad, handsome face. His hair was a tangled mess. There was a smudge of earth on his cheek.

"Why don't you write her a letter? Tell her how hurt he is," Mr. Buckle said.

"That's a thought," Stanford said, moving closer, then

sitting up and straddling his lover at the waist. "I think she should know."

He hovered over him, smiling, then settled back, manipulating his passion, slowly guiding them both to that shared place of abandon.

"What will you do when I leave?" Stanford said. "Replace me?"

Mr. Buckle was gasping now, as Stanford leaned back pressing both hands into the wet and succulent earth, rising and falling in rhythm, not waiting for an answer, instead throwing his head back and looking up through the scattering and sunburnt leaves at his own bright and formidable future, which he knew would be quite golden.

15

Richard, St. Louis, 1906

It was not a large or grand cemetery, St. Bridgit's, but it was old.

The souls crammed in narrow unkempt graves were of another century, a dank time, and the men, women and babies (there were many babies, Richard noticed) were very much of the earth. They had lived in dirt, rolled in it, yanked mud-splattered turnips from their rank little yards on Allemania or Bond Street or by the River des Peres. These graves were for the poorest of the poor.

Richard was not tasked with tending these graves, just digging new ones and making sure the local punks didn't destroy anything. He cared for all of the graves though, out of a deep respect for the dead. He cleared the weeds, scrubbed the cracked and tarnished headstones (the infants' graves, those still-born he dealt with most tenderly). He saw it as his penance, which gave him the drive to work all day and long into the night, earth staining his hands, sinking deep under his nails, keeping him swathed in and close to an endless grief. He created small crosses from branches and twigs tied with twine and placed them on the graves.

He'd written his parents and told them of Rolf's terrible death. They'd written back, asking him to come home, but he knew he would stay in America. He would never leave Rolf, never abandon the journey they had begun together.

He rented a room in the attic of a cement house on Allemania Street, which faced the cemetery. His room had a portal shaped window that looked out onto the grave yard, and he liked this view, this god-like perch of his, where he could keep an eye under a hallowed moon of those souls he tended. Mrs. Schuller, a round and cheerful German widow, lived alone in the house, renting the attic and offering dinner nightly. She made potato pancakes, hand rolled egg noodles, roasts and many, many cookies. It was these nightly feasts that drew Richard reluctantly out of his depression. That and the plum cake he found.

It was February dusk. The sky was hard and gray, tarnished as a tombstone. Snow was likely. He spied the bundle on a grave under the huge looming oak tree at the cemetery's north end. The tree shot up, pale and bony, branches growing from an unwieldy trunk, an ancient thing rising. He thought at first it was an abandoned infant so he ran to it. But it was only a loaf pan, wrapped in a white cloth. He picked it up. It was warm.

Richard looked around, then up at his own window. A new wind howled, and he sat on the ground and dug his hand into the pan, and ate half of the plum cake, deciding it must be from Mrs. Schuller. Later, at dinner, he thanked her for the cake and she said he spoke nonsense. She left no cake; it was clearly a trick of a wandering ghost or demon.

"I hope you didn't eat it," she said, serving him pork chops, homemade apple sauce, egg noodles with gravy and warm biscuits. "There are things not to be ignored in a place like that. There are things not to be fooled with."

That night, Richard sat up in his room, watching the graveyard through the portal window, particularly the spot under the oak. The snow had grown heavy, delicate white shreds mixing with slags of ice. He dozed sitting up, remembering that awful night in the woods, the jagged metal saw and his view of Rolf forever eclipsed by a thundering storm beating at him from the heavens.

When he woke, the cemetery was blanketed white. He glimpsed a pale figure darting past the oak, disappearing into dawn's mist. He shivered but not with fear, more a sense of discovery, a feeling that something was about to happen.

16

Cal, St. Louis, 1952

The evening sky, which a moment ago had been soft and dusky, held a new threat.

From their covered back porch, Cal and Josie watched storm clouds tremble in from the west. The procession was sluggish, as if nothing could move fast in the dreadful July heat. The clouds were as black as wet Missouri mud. The sky directly above them held onto a diminishing blue, that sharp late-evening blue that would soon be swallowed whole by the darkness. For a brief moment, Cal remembered flying a one-seater in the war, tearing through high cirrus. He turned to Josie.

"Storm's coming. It will cool things down."

"Hmmm…" Josie said, pursing her lips and holding onto the phrase like a slowly fading musical note.

That sound used to be like a melody to Cal, filled with wonder and whimsy, but now he knew it was a sign that she was getting riled. Something was coming. She was gathering an idea in her mind. There would likely be trouble.

Cal had set up two lawn chairs on the porch next to a crib where their son Stanford slept.

A small electric fan blew air onto the baby. Cal had laid the concrete for the new porch that summer, hoping it would make Josie happy. He'd also bought a bird bath and set it in the yard for her to look at. Josie had made that sound, her drawn out "hmmm," then asked him why he thought she wanted to watch a bird take a bath.

The air was still and heavy. A stretch of deep humidity before the storm. Cal looked at the horizon, and thought the approaching clouds looked like dirty cotton balls yanked violently from their stem, jagged and oddly shaped, cut up around the seams, butting edge to edge and massing slowly into big stormy continents. He was hoping that the rain would soften everything, including Josie.

Josie was wearing a floral cotton dress she called her hothouse throwaway. He thought she looked great, her hair piled on her head, her face glistening with sweat. The dress reminded him of something his mother would make but he didn't mention that. The head on his glass of beer had died. Josie sipped her warm wine.

"It's a nice night," Cal said.

Josie sighed.

"Cal, it's like a jungle in the house. We need central air conditioning."

So that's it, he thought. They'd been through this half a dozen times. The fact was they couldn't afford central air conditioning. But Josie was relentless once she got an idea in her head, whether it made sense or not.

There was a hard knock of distant thunder, and Cal wished the rain would hurry up. It would change things. It would move things along.

"We can barely sleep at night in this heat," Josie said.

"The summer's half gone," he said. "Maybe next year."

There was a light pick up in the wind and several loud

rumbles of thunder. Josie stood and made a growling, exasperated sound that came from deep in her throat. It was a sound he hated because it meant she was hurting, that she was angry, and that they were far from settled on this subject.

"Damn it, Cal," she said, turning away.

Her dress had thin straps and scooped down in the back, showing off her beautiful, suntanned shoulders. He wanted to get up and plant a few kisses on his favorite spot on the nape of her neck but he was afraid it might rile her more. Lightning cut across the sky, then thunder, then a wind. They were on the brink. The temperature would drop. A solid downpour would start soon, that hard rhythm of rain, softening everything. Cal loved the sound and the scent of rain, the hush of it. *Hurry up and rain!* he thought.

Josie began quietly, tilting her head to one side, keeping her back to him.

"You leave before seven now. You used to stay for breakfast. I'm in the house with the baby for…"she sighed and turned to the crib. "Twelve hours. Just him and me. He's such a good boy. Sleeps through this heat. You're not here, Cal. You don't know."

"Come on Josie, the mill took on two huge jobs," he said.

"It's not about the mill," she said.

"What?"

"Forget it, Cal," she said.

She stepped to the crib, checking the baby, then went into the house. There was a long row of lattice windows looking from the porch into the kitchen. He saw her pouring more wine. His boy was quiet.

"You don't mind the heat do you, Stan?" he said.

In the distance, lightning streaked again across the sky.

The trees in the nearby woods just over the hill by the two-lane road swayed. It would burst any minute. Cal looked up. There was nothing separating the clouds; it was one dark mass.

"Come on," he said. "Do something. What are you waiting for?"

He glanced back through the lattice windows. Josie was standing in the kitchen not moving. *What in the hell is she doing now?* he thought, turning back to the sky, angry, tired of waiting for the rain. He wished the clouds would rip open and let all that storm rage, give it up completely so he'd have that coolness, that constant sound of a downpour.

The rain would send him inside and the wind would blow full through the windows and Josie would feel the wind and be happy again. Maybe they'd go to bed early and make love and he'd get Josie some ice cream and they'd make up. He could rub ice on her neck and she'd move her face against his cheek like she used to.

The high grass in the empty plot next to their house blew sideways with a new gust. The grass was wild, reedy and overgrown. Josie didn't like that. She said it looked like a trash lot.

Josie knocked on the window behind him. She was pointing into the high grass. He smiled and she hit the window again. Stanford woke up and began to fuss in his crib. Josie knocked harder, pointing.

Cal stood up and saw what she saw, and knew it was not good. The fox, the silver headed hunter, was back. He'd seen the animal the other night scrounging for food but he hadn't mentioned it. Josie had developed a holy terror of foxes and raccoons since they'd moved into the house. It was a fear Cal never understood so he ignored it, hoping it would disappear. He knew that once they plowed over the woods the foxes and raccoons would scram. They were harmless. Back on Allemania he used to feed the possums behind their house.

Josie was still knocking on the window and Stanford was awake, but not crying. The baby was making light cheerful noises, which made Cal laugh. The wind had picked up again and with that, thunder. Cal turned to the window and smiled at Josie.

"It's all right, come on out," he said.

She disappeared and he watched the little fox as the rain finally began, a full on and immediate torrent. The onslaught was the only sound now and its lulling power quieted Stanford. The wind and rain had cooled things considerably and there was a mist blowing in. He turned and looked down at his son, who smiled up at him, his forehead wet with spray.

When he turned back he saw her, out in the rain, not under the cover of the porch but on the blacktop driveway that ran along the side of the house and bordered the neighbor's plot. She had his hunting rifle on her shoulder and her hair hung wet on her back and the flower dress was sheer in the rain and he could see the beautiful curve of her hips and he started to shout but his voice was obliterated with a deafening clap of thunder and then—the sound of a shot.

Stanford was sitting up in the crib reaching for him but Cal ran to Josie and tried to grab the gun from her, but she wouldn't let it go. They both held it facing one another and her eyes were wild and her breasts shone through the soaked dress and she started yelling.

"You said they would tear that all down, you said it was all changing, that's what you said, Cal!"

There was another hard knock of thunder and her lips pulled back in a terrible grimace. Then she let go of the gun and ran in the house. He walked over to the high grass, where the fox lay, part of its skull blown off, blood running into the earth, then onto their blacktop. He wondered where she'd learned to shoot. She had damn good aim.

He stood in the rain awhile, and he wondered if it was all ruined, if she was too far gone for the night to be salvaged. Still, he yearned to kiss that soft spot on her neck. He wondered what he might say to her, and he was not sure what to do. The storm came on harder for a moment, then a light hail, and he was afraid to turn around, strangely afraid to face her, or worse yet, afraid she might have vanished with the storm. He heard the door open.

"Come in, bring the baby, dear God, Cal," she yelled.

Cal was soaked from the downpour. He looked up. There was clear sky in the distance. Storms came and went fast in Missouri. It would all be blue again soon, until the next one.

He went to the porch and lifted his son, who frowned at him. Cal held him close, patting his back and comforting him as he cooed, wishing he could think of some way to comfort Josie. He looked through the lattice window for his wife, but he could not see her.

17

Stanford and Bo lay shirtless on the banks of the Mississippi River, pale backs pressed against the cobblestones that formed the shore. The St. Louis Arch soared behind them, a towering silver specter, the gateway to the west. They could see Illinois across the water. It was nearly dawn and 102 degrees.

They were going back to New York City in the morning, but not as lovers. School was done and they were starting a real estate business. Bo draped his leg over the top of Stanford's thigh.

"We can still fuck sometimes, right?" Bo said.

"No," Stanford said softly.

Bo stood up and went to the river's edge. He dipped his hand into the brown water, splashing his shoulders.

"That's disgusting," Stanford said.

"Fucking?"

"The river. Get away from there."

"You worry too much," Bo said.

It was true. Stanford analyzed and assessed the risk of every moment, obsessing over shreds of detail, managing his secretly raging superstitions. Bo took risks and followed his gut. Their first big business deal, buying a condemned building on Manhattan's east side for next to nothing, was handled by Bo during a late-night game of poker. Stanford had been studying for finals. Within a year, they'd demolished and sold the building at a whopping profit.

Bo liked people, and people liked Bo. Stanford was better alone, computing risk analysis, investing quietly and resolving road blocks. Over the past four years, they'd already amassed a good deal of money, exploiting one another's peculiarities and strengths. They'd also had a great deal of really good sex.

Stanford watched Bo, who sat at the river's edge, his back, that sweeping hard warrior's back, arched and wing-like. He was a thing of beauty, a wildly distracting beast of a lover. Stanford wondered if he could truly stick to his guns, and say no to their intense sensual bond. It was something that had begun slowly and grown over time into a consuming addiction.

Their most intimate moments always left Stanford shattered, drowning in a lush and weakened place. Stanford knew that if they continued as lovers, he would become a lesser thing, a shell of himself, a lowly and wavering creature reaching forward to get more of the nectar. He had deep urges to devour Bo, dreams where his jaw became an ocean and he swallowed Bo whole. His determination to focus and succeed in business had set him on a new course. That was why they could not be lovers—or at least that's what he told himself. In truth, he wondered if he was just too weak to love deeply, if his intense fear of losing what was precious to him made it impossible to give into anything fully.

"So can we keep fucking a little, right?" Bo said, going to sit beside Stanford.

"Business comes first. Always," Stanford said. "We've got a lot at stake."

"You got the brains, I got the big balls. We're gonna knock New York on its ass," Bo said.

Slight trembling drops of river water glided off Bo's shoulder. Stanford wanted to lean in, to smell Bo, to taste the dirty water. But he did not. Things had to change.

"When are you going to tell me what's in the case?" Bo said.

Stanford waited. He could be the tease for once, let Bo linger in wonder. He put his palm on the top of the black case at his side.

"Are you sure you're ready?" Stanford said.

"It can't be a rifle. Too small," Bo said.

"Shut your eyes," Stanford said. "And lie back."

Bo did as he was told and Stanford opened the case. He gently lifted out the trumpet, which his father had given him on his twelfth birthday, handed down from his Uncle Rolf. He brought it to his lips. The metal nipple had an ancient taste of tin. It was an old thing, though still shone golden in the soft morning light. He pursed his lips and blew.

Bo sat up, startled by the loud and bellowing blast.

"What is that?"

"Be quiet," Stanford said.

He blew again, pressing one of the knobs on the instrument's spine.

"That sounds like something trapped!" Bo said. "Stop!"

Stanford took a deep breath and blew once more, pressing out air for as long as he could. He finished and held the trumpet in his lap.

"It's our swan song," Stanford said. "A song to end one

thing and start another."

"Don't do that again," Bo said. "It's horrible."

"I just need a few lessons. It's a family heirloom," Stanford said. "I'm taking it to New York for good luck."

"Can I try?" Bo said.

Stanford looked at the golden trumpet. He could see his marred and imperfect reflection in its side.

"No. Only I can play it. And my son someday."

"You are having a son?" Bo said.

"Maybe," Stanford said.

"Isn't a swan song a final act?"

"Yes,"

"So all business in New York, but we still have tonight," Bo said.

Bo stood up, glanced around, then unbuttoned his pants. He slid them off and Stanford knew he was lost.

Things would change in New York but this was St. Louis and there was the wrecked Mississippi, a river that had made men rich, devoured them, that saw a city soar and crash.

He laid down his great uncle's trumpet and reached forward, cheek on thigh, reckless scents and abandon, losing all sense of himself, surrendering just for now.

18

Richard, St. Louis, 1906

Richard spent time alone at the grave, under the mighty oak tree. Nothing had happened since he'd found the plum cake.

Still, after work, under a bold moon in whose hallowed and pocked face he imagined the visage of a wild boar, he sat and waited. It was ripping cold, and he could see from where he sat the lighted window of his attic room, his refuge. Each night, despite the cold, he lingered. Hours went by. Snow came. He imagined things rustling, as if Rolf were floating just above him.

The depth of grief that had brought him to St. Louis slowly began to melt, eased by his first hungry bites of the gifted plum cake, that magic of flour, sugar and butter. As he waited, he began to set his sights on something coming, rather than that which was gone. For several nights, he shivered, and he waited and more than once Mrs. Schuller said he was foolish and quite possibly mad.

Then one day, on the grave, sat fist-sized muffins stuffed with pieces of apple and topped with sugar and cinnamon. The next day was a lacework apple pie, then a plate of horn shaped cookies, then a date prune pudding, then Emma.

It was a cold morning and Richard was dressed for digging, bundled deep and wrapped up. He saw her as he came out of Mrs. Sculler's house and approached the cemetery. She was sitting on the grave where the treats had been left, under the oak. He thought, *That's her. I could fit her in the palm of my hand.*

She was underdressed in a white peasant smock and strange green shoes with heels, a green knitted hat and a thin emerald-colored scarf that blew up over her head like a kite tail yanked skyward. Her hair was white blonde and scattered with the strong wind and he was afraid she could be pulled up into the sky, gone forever.

He walked quickly, removing his heavy coat lined with fur hides. She was facing away from him. He came behind her and he put the coat over her shoulders and it nearly swallowed her whole. He looked down at her, and thought, *This is how the oak looks down at me, I am small to that and she is small to me.*

She turned fast, overwhelmed now by Richard's coat, he looming and strong in a heavy wool undershirt and ratted fur hat. She smiled and said nothing. He was grateful as his English was so poor he was frightened that he may say the wrong thing and scare her away. Freckles like pale scattered stars covered her pixie face. He wanted to say *you are an angel* but he could not cipher that in his mind so he simply said "heaven."

She did not stop smiling and took his large hands in hers, that green scarf still sailing upward with the wind. She guided him away from the grave, past Mrs. Schuller's to a house at the end of Allemania Street whose windows had bright red shutters. He realized he had never ventured down the street, always turned straight for the graves.

She is taking me back to life, he thought.

She brought him into the house, and they sat down to eat a lunch that was already prepared and set out, as if she knew the future, as if she knew he would come to her.

19

Cal, St. Louis, 1959

Minnie's road house sold fried brain sandwiches and a 25-cent glass of beer.

Cal and his poker buddies Sal, Floyd and "bull dog" Norman spent a lot of Saturday nights drinking there after the war, and still met at Minnie's to play cards once a month, only now they brought their wives.

The strip of Gravois Road where Minnie's stood had seen trouble. Stores had come and gone, a liquor shop had been ripped apart by a tornado, but Minnie's was indestructible. It was made of stone, and sat on a hill across from a Dairy Queen. It had a dirt parking lot, a good juke box, and sturdy tables for card playing.

Josie told Cal she hated Minnie's the first time they went, but Cal convinced her it was a "boy's" tradition and she needed to get along with his friends' wives, Sissy, Carole and Rosemary. Sissy was built like a Vegas show girl, dressed like a society woman and laughed at everything the men said. Carole was timid with dyed red hair and a squeaky voice. And Rosemary was busty, funny and slightly overweight.

It was just past midnight and Cal was winning. Floyd and Sal had already dropped out of the hand. Norm threw down his cards in defeat and finally lit the cigar clenched between his teeth. Norm had a perfect square jaw, which is why they called him bull dog, plus he liked to bark when he got drunk. Sissy, his wife, told everyone he was hilarious. Call raked in the pot and Floyd shuffled the cards.

It was August and so hot that they got used to warm beer and sweating. The door was kept open, giving a view of the parking lot. Josie stood in the doorway looking at Cal. She'd been acting strange all night. Refusing to sit and play gin rummy with the rest of the girls, abandoning her usual soda for several gin and tonics. Sis had called her back to the table several times, then gave up. The ladies often gossiped amongst themselves about Josie's being stuck up and moody.

"She thinks being a Beddenfield makes her special," Sis said, dealing a hand.

Josie had wandered out to the parking lot and back several times in the past hour.

"Dealers choice, let's play Twenty One, gentlemen," Floyd said at the men's table.

Floyd was easy going and the biggest of their group. He was six foot four and when he stood up to stretch Cal thought of the towering black jack oaks at his grandfather's summer house. Sal was the opposite. Barely five foot four and as round as a bowling ball. Cal was dealt two tens. He'd play it easy and see what he could raise from the boys.

Josie was still in the doorway. She hadn't moved. Headlights from passing cars shined into the place, a fast dissolving brightness. The light curled around Josie and Cal admired her in that flowered dress, cinched at the waist with a pink ribbon, her hair piled up like she was going somewhere important. She was wearing pink high heels, something he hadn't noticed but couldn't miss now. She looked tall and regal standing there, her head cocked to one side, watching him, a glass of gin in her hand. She lifted her hand and held it aloft and as another headlight swept over her, he thought he saw her lips move but then the light was gone. She waved to him, then turned and disappeared into the parking lot.

"You still with us, Cal?" Floyd said.

Another passing car lit the empty doorway, Sis started to laugh at the ladies' table, a shrill sound, and Cal looked at his winning cards, then threw them on the table.

"I'm out," he said. "Be right back."

As he stood up, he had an odd sensation, a slightly sick feeling in his belly, and a flash of memory as he made his way to the wide-open door. He thought of the way the door flew open and stayed open that night in the drug store, the blue pistols blazing, men falling dead and him holding onto a blue feather in his pocket, a feather he took with him to the war but had forgotten about ever since. He did not know where he'd put it. He was also struck with an odd urgency and his heart raced as he went to find Josie.

Out in the parking lot, he saw her standing alone, leaning on the hood of their car, smoking a cigarette. She had quit smoking last year. He didn't know she'd started up again. He moved toward her and she watched him. He got to her and thought to reach out and touch her cheek, but he didn't.

"Did you win?" she said.

"Mostly," he said.

He was struck by her slow movement, how she lifted the cigarette to her lips, and her sense of calm. She was a plucky girl, he always told her that, and he was used to her asking for things, telling him what they needed to do next. Dreaming about things. She was staring at him, which made him uncomfortable.

"Are you ready to leave?" he said.

She was still looking at him and he did not look away. They stood that way, staring at one another, and there was no breeze and the heat was relentless. Cal's collar was wet with sweat. He was frightened but of what he could not tell.

"Are you all right?" he said. "We can go."

She parted her lips and took in a breath. Then she smiled and finally looked away.

"I was just thinking about something," she said. "Something on my mind."

She brought the glass of gin to her lips, which were painted a peach color. He hadn't noticed that either. She sipped her drink. He waited, thinking she would go on. It wasn't like her to hold back. Cal shifted on his feet, side to side. She looked away and spoke in a near whisper.

"My father always said to me, you need to settle down Josie. But it's just that I'm not…"

A car drove by, windows open, and voices roared from the front seat, loud bright voices and a disappearing sound of laughter, and Cal couldn't hear what Josie was saying. Then it was quiet. The noisy car was gone, the street empty, and he felt he'd missed something important. She was looking at him. Cal thought he should ask her again if she was all right, and what it was it she had said, but he just stood still waiting. She dropped her cigarette and kept her head down and reached out to take his hand in hers. She was very quietly crying.

Sis stepped out into the parking lot.

"Let's get a rocky road sundae!" Sis yelled and waved from the doorway. The group always went for sundaes at the

Dairy Queen after cards. Sis had a terrible sweet tooth, she told everyone, adding that Norm was so sweet she didn't know why she needed more sugar.

"With whipped cream. We gotta eat it fast in this heat!" Sis said.

Cal let go of Josie's hand to wave to Sis, watching the rest of them emerge. When he turned back Josie was already in the car. She had lit another cigarette and that was all he could see, that dim red glow. He felt something had just happened, but he figured he could bring it up later, now that everyone was swarming their car, laughing. Maybe she was pregnant again; that made her moody. He got in and started the car and did not say anything and they drove across the road to the Dairy Queen.

At Sis' insistence, they all ate rocky road sundaes.

20

Stanford, Manhattan, 1982

Stanford and Bo were deep into the bowels of the Mud Club, on an oversized sofa-like platform covered with multi-colored fake fur. Above their heads hung shimmering strands of silver beads and several plastic skulls. The walls were black. The music was cacophonous.

Stanford spotted his mother at the far end of the club edging through Amazonian women in leopard bikinis and stilettos, men in leather and satin, couples gyrating to Animal X.

He had hoped she wouldn't show up. Or that if she did, she'd face the insanity that was the hyper-trendy and equally trashy Mud Club and run. But there she was, in a robin's egg blue Chanel suit, her dark hair sprayed up, making her way through the throng, smiling as if at afternoon tea. While he had initially applauded his mother's quest for independence when she left Missouri for Paris, the slow decline of his father, the man's aching despair, created a new bond between father and son. Stanford felt terrible for his father, and began to blame his mother.

He saw her annually at Christmas, for a cool subdued supper in either Paris or New York, and things remained civil. But year by year, his unrest rose bile-like and sour, until in a drunken moment he had called her and demanded she come to see him, that he had something to tell her. The next morning, reeling with a hangover, he prayed she'd ignored his rant. He couldn't piece together what his scotch-fueled mind felt so compelled to tell her. His feelings were nothing more than a jumble of resentments. But a week later, she announced her visit. Bo had suggested he simply tell her not to come. Instead he decided to set a meeting at a dank, inappropriate spot, drink a lot before she arrived, and hope she'd step in the door and turn right around and leave.

"Oh God," Stanford said.

"Relax," Bo said. "Don't make it a bigger deal than it needs to be."

Bo swung his legs over the edge of the platform, nearly upending a small table with a pitcher of blue martinis. He was wearing tight white pants, several gold chains and nothing else.

"Josie!" Bo yelled.

His mother graciously took in his friend's hug, not flinching as Bo's lean, tan and muscled chest pressed against her pale blue finery. The two of them had always gotten along. Stanford wished Bo had not come.

Stanford did not move. His mother made her way to his side of the platform, and sat on the edge. She leaned toward him, her pink lips barely grazing his cheek, which was misty with sweat.

"It's good to see you," she said, speaking loudly and with distinction.

"Thanks for coming," he said.

A man wearing hot pants and a paper crown was moving quickly toward them. At the last moment he stopped and turned back. They sat listening to shouts, rank lyrics and metallic music, along with some howling.

"Well…" Josie said. "It's loud."

Bo laughed and clapped his hands. Stanford sat stiffly, increasingly uncomfortable. A mild anger was welling up. He downed his drink.

"I like it here," he said loudly.

Two young women wearing white wigs, cigarettes dangling from pink lips, thin champagne flutes in hand, moved by slowly and cautiously on roller skates.

They edged past Bo, toward Stanford and Josie, inch by inch. One of the girls turned to Josie as she passed and screamed, "Love the Chanel!"

The girls passed, Bo began to sing along with the music and they sat a while longer, then his mother stood up sharply. She cleared her throat, and shouted over the music.

"Why don't we go somewhere to eat? It's just too loud in here to talk. I can go ahead and you can join me. How would that be?"

A blinking strobe light began, the crowd cooed, and Stanford saw her dissolve from light to dark, appearing, vanishing, appearing again. He moved off of the platform and stood near her.

"No," he said. "I've got something to say."

He faced her. The strobe was dizzying, her taut face still dissolving and emerging. He felt a surge of anger and grief, knowing that he wanted to speak not for just himself but for his father, deciphering and expressing a lingering anguish the two men shared.

"You don't get to leave us this time, mother," Stanford said. "You can't just run away."

Josie took Stanford's hands, but he pulled them away. She took them up again and held tight, squeezing, and Stanford tried to locate the words, the things he no longer wanted to accept about the past, but nothing came together. Josie leaned in closer.

"What is it, Stanford?" she said.

"Why do you hate him?' he said.

Josie let go of his hands, and with that movement, it was as if her entire form deflated and shrank. She brought her hand to her lips, began to speak, then quickly wrapped her arms around her son, hugging him tightly, not letting go.

Stanford could smell her perfume, and it was a familiar scent, something he knew, and he let his head sink into her shoulder, into that aroma, and looking past her at the mad tangle of nothingness, of plastic, sequins, thighs and smoke, he let himself cry, not needing to know why.

21

Cal, St. Louis, 1967

Cal steered the silver nose of the two-seater aircraft higher, wheels up with a clear shot ascending to a stark blue sky.

He only flew on clear days and never alone. His war memories—angrily cutting into clouds talking to himself—were worn but never gone. The plane was slowly climbing, that hard noise of rushing air sending him soaring, this incredible sensation broken only by Stanford's scream.

"Wooooooo!"

It was a raw howling. Stanford had never been on a flight, had never shown any interest in his father's hobby. It was his sixteenth birthday and to Cal's surprise, he'd asked to go flying.

Cal took the plane higher, imagining his son's face behind him in the two-seater plane. They would stay fairly low, so Stanford could take in the landscape. They would fly over Rolf's Retreat, and further to the stretch of scarred and pockmarked land that had once been rich with timber, over the ruins of the once thriving lumber camp that his father had worked at so many years ago. And over the hard and barren spot that had gone damp with Uncle Rolf's blood one Christmas Eve.

"Can you teach me to fly?" Stanford yelled.

He had told his son it would be loud, difficult to communicate. He raised a hand to let him know he heard. Cal felt weak and a little light headed as they rose. He had not flown much lately. On occasion a business client wanted a ride. Josie refused to even look at the plane after he bought it a few years back. She hated the idea of him risking his life for a thrill, as she put it. The first time he went up was the first time she went away.

"Gone to Milan," was all the note said.

He'd come back from flying, ruddy cheeked and feeling vital, having scraped away a few years of dry business meetings and number crunching, summoning a sense of discovery he thought he'd left behind years ago in Hawaii. He'd wanted to tell her about it, to at last talk honestly about the slowly rising tide of subtle disagreements that had come between them.

"Gone to Milan."

She'd returned in a week. No explanation. He refused to ask her, refused to acknowledge her selfish acting out. After that, with each flight came a price. "Gone to Paris." "Gone to Rome."

He wondered if she'd be gone when they got back today, or if Stanford's planned birthday dinner would stifle her.

"Rolf's!" Stanford yelled.

Cal slowed and leveled, circling his father's summer place, so small from above and somehow simple and without memories, as if it was brand new and a spot he'd never been to. The lake looked still with a gentle mist rising.

They flew on, over flat lands, fallow and empty lands, things unsown and dreary in their emptiness, he thought.

"Happy birthday, son," Cal said, unsure if Stanford heard

him.

"I'm going to buy a plane," Stanford shouted over the engine's roar. "I can fly you and Grandpa Richard and Granny Emma somewhere!"

In the distance, as they made a turn, Cal spotted a singular farm house and a barn. There were so few in this area since the timber yards shut down. Cal saw a figure emerge from the house, a woman, stepping out and waiting there, and he imagined it was Josie who would look up and wave, calling them down, waving to them with absolute joy. He made the turn and the vision was gone.

"Thanks, Dad!" Stanford yelled.

Cal could not speak, overwhelmed with a sudden rush of memory, of Josie sitting next to him in the Chevy, arguing about a name, asking for a Coke with shaved ice, knowing their future was bright and limitless.

22

Richard, Missouri, 1933

When together, the family spent most of their time in the kitchen, which Emma said was the heart of the small house at the end of Allemania. It was the brightest room, facing the back yard, with both a window and a door with three glass panes to draw light. They met nightly for dinner around the square table which Richard had built. It was knotty pine, painted bright white.

Richard sat at the head, Cal on one side. There was an empty chair at the opposite end with a hand sewn lace doily draped across the back and a small feather pillow on the seat for Emma, who rarely sat, rather spent her time singing and cooking at the porcelain cast iron stove, talking in low whispers the two did not pay much attention to.

It was Sunday. They feasted on a roast, new potatoes and carrots from the small back garden. It was Richard's birthday. It was a warm summer evening and Emma was barefoot carrying a plum cake on a fine china plate, a candle lit in its center. She set it on the table, gave Richard a kiss on the cheek and he blew it out. Emma clapped and set about serving.

"Are you ready?" she said.

She gave them each a fat slab of the cake, then sat and

tasted it herself. Richard watched her, those same bird-like movements he'd fallen for, even from a distance, the day he witnessed her in the graveyard. To him, she had not changed a lick and as stern as he could be with his son, as tired as he was from long days working as a cement layer and carpenter, when he looked at her, he was filled with both overwhelming joy and a shivering grief at the thought of ever losing her. She was his light.

She took his hand and smiled at him. He knew what was coming. Birthdays belonged to Emma. Cal was busy devouring the dense cake packed with fresh plums, topped with a sweet almond icing.

"Your mother asked you a question, Cal," Ricard said.

Cal set down his fork and sat up straight. He turned to face his mother who had a nibble of plum cake perched on the edge of a tiny spoon. Emma laughed, a high chirping laugh. She rarely had anyone's attention, so fully at least.

"Who would like to start?" she said, swallowing the sweet nibble.

"Well," Cal said. "I think..."

Richard turned to his son.

"*Denke nicht Sohn. Kennt,*" Richard said first in German, then, "Do not think son. Know."

Cal did not look directly at his father. They had fought recently, in hushed tones but still with fervor, over Cal's defiantly continuing to do stray jobs with the Eagan Rats. Richard never forgave himself for getting his son involved with those no goods. He regretted his short0lived adventure in bootlegging and hated the dark undercurrent and stain it had left on his son.

"I'm going to fly planes," Cal said.

Emma clapped her hands, jumped from her seat and went to Cal, kissing his cheek.

"Soar near the heavens, don't ever be afraid to fly higher, what is here on the ground is passing," she said.

Richard was satisfied. Cal was not book smart, but piloting could be a talent born of instinct and courage, and his son had both. He was a fearless young man, and he knew what he wanted, in some ways, more so than Richard ever had. A few years back, Cal had spent hours helping his father improve his English, revealing a fierce determination that startled Richard.

Emma stood.

"And that dream, now spoken on this special day, has power. Now you, Richard," Emma said.

He did not put much stock in Emma's soothsaying, though her predictions often came true, her herbal brews cured his ailments, and the beauty of her heart was like a wreath of gentle flowers that never left his chest.

"My dream is here," he said.

He went to Emma, towering over her, and lifted her up, holding her tightly, kissing her cheek, then keeping her aloft, rocking gently, taking in the scent of her, the fullness of her love, the beauty of what she was to him.

23

The strip stretched deep into a seamless desert, spiked with fake light and glitter, some ungodly wonderland wielding a frenetic sense of emptiness and urgency. From on high, in a sleek and soundless penthouse suite, Stanford imagined the landscape alive with the cries and howls of lost souls. He was terribly jet lagged and had no appetite. His father had died a year ago on this night. He lay on the giant bed, listening to a voice message from Bo.

"Stan hey, remember that moon baby?"

Bo sounded very drunk. His voice was hollow, ragged. Music droned in the background, a jungle beat.

"Fucking under that moon baby. We were so dumb. You made me swim in the fucking frozen lake. Hey, I'm sorry I can't see you this year like always but you can't, I can't be what...."

There was a clattering sound, as if Bo had dropped the phone, and Stanford deleted the message. He and Bo, long-time business partners and friends, still met every Thanksgiving. But this year Bo had other plans. And Stanford had flown to Vegas on a whim.

There was a rumbling above. The November night was warm and clear so it couldn't be a storm. Stanford stayed on the top floor at hotels, always. He could not abide anyone above him, for he knew dark spirits began below, under, beneath. One was always safer closer to the sky, his Granny Emma told him.

Restless, he decided to go out. He had never been to old Vegas, and had read about a gay dive-bar called Snicks. He had his driver drop him in front of the bar and wait in the parking lot.

It was a boxy joint with cheap metal siding and a flashing Snicks sign on its low roof. It looked more like a derelict convenience store than a desert roadside hangout. Inside, things were dark. A line of wood booths, a long rambling bar, a juke box. The place was empty, save for a bartender and one shirtless young man alone in a back booth shuffling a pack of large colorful cards. The young man looked up and stared at Stanford. Stanford went to the booth.

"I knew it, I just knew it. The cards told me a dark stranger would come into my life," the young man said. "Sit down."

Stanford sat. The young man was a pale redhead. His long hair was shining with oil and pushed back in a thick mess. He was sinewy, lean, and well built. He was young, maybe twenty, Stanford thought.

"I told my friend Edna that something was coming for me today," he said. "Didn't I, Boss? Tonight is the night."

Boss was a heavy-set bald man in a black T-shirt tending bar. He grunted. The young man laid out five tarot cards.

"I'm getting a beer," Stanford said. "Do you want something?"

"Gin on ice," the young man said.

He looked up. His eyes were startling green, soft emeralds. Stanford got the drinks. He sat and the redhead lifted each large colorful card and placed it on top of the card next to it until they made a neat stack. Stanford liked redheads. He always had. The young man's chest was very pale and smooth, which he also liked. He hadn't been looking tonight but here it was. And he hadn't had sex for a long time. And he was pissed at Bo.

"I knew you'd come," the young man said.

Boss snorted from the bar.

"He bothering you, mister?" Boss said. "He's a little crazy."

"We're all right," Stanford said.

The young man put his palms on the table, and took a deep breath. He seemed to be taking the cards very seriously. He laid several more out, glancing up at Stanford. Then he set down the deck.

"Can I have your palms?" the young man said. "I'm not really feeling these cards."

He smiled, gently, and for a moment Stanford got lost in those emerald eyes. He gave up his palms. The redhead studied his palms, then ran one finger along the center of each.

"You don't work with these hands," he said. "But you have been read before. Somebody in your life. Somebody like me. A real fortune teller."

Stanford liked the feel of the young man's finger running across his palm.

"Let's go," Stanford said. "I'm hungry."

He got up and the shirtless redhead did not move.

"What else are you doing tonight?" Stanford said, turning and striding out. "Come on."

"You have a point," the redhead said, following.

"Where is your shirt?" Stanford said.

"That's a long story," the redhead said.

"See you tomorrow, Sam," Boss said.

At the door, the re head turned.

"Maybe," he said.

"Your name is Sam?" Stanford said.

"Yes. My stage name is Bolt."

"What stage?"

"I used to do readings in the lobby of the Sands but that didn't quite work out."

"We can go to my hotel," said Stanford.

Back at the hotel, Sam laid his entire tarot card deck on the hotel suite's king-sized bed while Stanford ordered room service. Sam did this with extreme precision, making sure the edge of each card butted the edge of its sister card, that the rows were symmetrical and perfectly even and that the story unfolding was pure.

Stanford dazzled at this delicacy and obsessive precision, but once he sidled next to his guest, stood shoulder to shoulder studying the wild purpled and thrusting imagery on the cards, something happened that couldn't be stopped. Sam reached out a long freckled arm to retrieve the first card. Watching, Stanford was electrified by the look of that arm, the perfection and immaculate skin tone, the branch-like reach of it. Things crashed in his brain, lusty memories of swimming with Bo years back, fucking through the years, frozen dangling tree limbs and icy howling moons and Stanford welled up with a new and inexhaustible lust that had lain dormant for months, and he could not stop himself from pushing Sam onto the bed and covering him with his body, the multi-colored soothsaying cards folding inward to touch their cheeks and curl under their arms as Stanford yanked at their clothing until they were naked.

As they made love, Sam took stray cards and pressed them on Stanford's face and belly and legs and Stanford went to many places, as orgasm hovered and lingered, guided by Sam's courtesan-like skill. Stanford fell fast and furious, and felt he was being devoured by a new state of sensuality both barbaric and mystical.

The wet of Sam's tongue on his thigh again brought back icy swims and the divine lust of early Bo, and that loss and grief too, and his father, dead now a year, and his hand cupping supple ass brought the hard sudden touch of timber and then those smells, multiple scents, of the mill and Mr. Buckle's muskiness and Granny Emma and more dreams he'd forgotten.

When he did finally climax, his back hot and wet, tarot cards matted to him, he was looking into Sam's eyes, for Sam was hovering over him riding, lips split wide open in a ferocious grin, skin translucent, tongue lolling and they both cut loose with deep animal cries, hard dark screaming that rose and rose and rose, until Sam fell onto Stanford and they lay still. The sun rose and just outside the window, Vegas seethed.

Sam flew back to New York with Stanford that day, after Stanford bought him several shirts and a suit. They spent days in bed in Stanford's Manhattan penthouse. Stanford asked Sam to move in, and Sam said yes.

24

Cal, St. Louis, 1969

Every thirteen years, the cicadas swarmed.

"It's that damn oak, maybe the ash tree, that's what draws the locusts," said Thornton Beddenfield, Josie's grandfather. "Cut them all down. Put in a swimming pool."

Cal and Thornton were on the back porch. The thrashing brood of insects had swallowed the town whole with their deafening cry that would last a solid week.

Thornton, in a white suit and wearing a white straw hat, mopped his forehead and swallowed his whiskey. He was a large man who had led an epic life. Despite his advanced age, he was a powerful presence and when he spoke, he did so with an authority born of privilege and great wealth. Cal took in the solemn night sky. Josie had been in Paris for a month.

"They're cicadas, not locusts," Cal said.

"Same thing. Bugs. All that noise so they can mate. Imagine if we did that sort of howling," Thornton said.

He swallowed his whiskey and turned to his son-in-law.

"You need to move back to Huntleigh. That's all she needs."

"I never lived in Huntleigh," Cal said.

"Semantics. We'd got a ripping country club. There's a

grand Victorian two story on Maple Drive for sale," Thornton said. "Josie would like it. Trust me. I know women. Don't buy into her nonsense. She'll be back any day."

Cal followed the sway of the snow-white hydrangea bushes lining his back yard, piercing the night, moving in motion to the rise and fall of the insects' song. He recalled the year Josie planted those.

"How's the boy?" Thornton said. "Still a problem?"

"He's going to New York to study business," Cal said. "He's doing fine."

There was a lull with the night cry, the chorus hushing.

"He's doing something all right. Did you sort out all that nonsense?" Thornton said.

Cal admired his son's drive, the intensity of his very singular passion. Stanford was smart, and knew exactly what he wanted in life. He trusted his son.

"Stanford knows what he's doing," Cal said.

Thornton stood and went to the edge of the porch. He was over six feet tall and still solidly put together, though hunching with the weight of age.

"I'm the reason those two young men aren't in jail," he said. "Rolling naked in the grass like mad dogs."

"They were swimming," Cal said.

Thornton turned and snorted, as the cicadas launched a new campaign of longing.

"That other boy's parents are a bit less Greek than you, Cal," he said. "I don't give two shits what that boy does, but he is your only heir. He needs to take his place at the mill and do the right thing. You should take a firmer hand with both of them."

"I doubt that is what Stanford will want to do," Cal said.

Cal stood up tentatively, as if the older man's shadow could swallow him whole. He never liked Josie's grandfather. Years ago, he had paid him back for the lumber they used to build the house. He didn't like owing him anything.

"You wait and see. New York is not easy on boys like him," Thornton said. "He'll be back after that city knocks some sense into him. You can quote me on that."

"I'd like to promote Mr. Buckle," Cal said.

Beyond the sound of the cicadas came the roar of a motor. Stanford pulled up on the side of the house. He drove an old Mustang convertible that he and his friend Bo had souped up.

"You're home early," Cal said.

Stanford moved toward them quickly.

"Just came by to get a suit. We're going swimming,"

"Oh dear God," said Thornton.

Stanford paused near the back door to the house, then turned to face his great-grandfather. Cal saw in his son a tilt of the head, an upward movement, a pressing of his shoulders ever so slightly backward that revealed a powerful and innate knowing. It was a look Josie had given him many times, a look that frightened him, a look he had tried not to see but now did see, did recall and missed with a deep and terrible longing.

Stanford's voice rang clear over the night sounds.

"I'm sure you swam in the river when you were young, great-grandfather. I'm sure you did at least that," Stanford said.

Thornton puffed his chest and made a sound, as if he would speak, but he did not speak. Stanford held the old man's stare until Thornton turned away, then he continued into the house and the two men regained their chairs on the porch, facing the shrubbery.

"Keep a close eye on him," Thornton said. "He thinks he knows more than he does."

Cal smiled, for he knew his son was capable of things he himself was not capable of; his son had a way of turning into not away from life. And for this he was grateful.

25

Stanford, Manhattan, 1992

Stanford moved powerfully through the water. There was a circular light glowing through fog. He swam harder, trying to reach the light as it dimmed. He looked up at shadows across the wavering blue. Then the water became clear and he saw her, tiny and bird-like Granny Emma, white hair flying, hands purple with plum stained reaching for him. He was drowning. He tried to swim up to her. Her lips were moving and she was speaking to him but he could not hear her. He swam harder, but the surface was impenetrable. He would die. Then she shook him.

"Stanford?"

It was Sam. They were in bed in their Manhattan penthouse. Stanford was wet with sweat.

"You were screaming," Sam said, holding him close.

As the dream faded, Stanford felt a lingering sense of foreboding, and was struck with a memory of Granny Emma speaking to him in the summer kitchen on his twelfth birthday, telling his fortune. He saw pale glimpses of that day, as if he were staring into a very bright light, blinded and only able to make out fading lines, images, things she'd said. Warnings. That was the day he rescued Bo.

"I was drowning," Stanford said. "What does that mean?"

Sam touched Stanford's face gently, then laughed.

"Hell if I know. Nothing I'd guess," he said.

Sam had revealed early in their relationship that he was a fake. He had no talent, no bright insight as a fortune teller. The Vegas act was a ruse. Stanford had confessed he was mildly disappointed, and told Sam about his Granny Emma, her soothsaying, how important she was to him. She had died years ago.

"She sounds remarkable," Sam had said, making Stanford find a photo of her.

They framed it and hung it in the kitchen, something Stanford had been too grieved to ever consider.

"Who were you yelling at?" Sam said.

Stanford shut his eyes and saw her there.

"It was Granny Emma," Stanford said.

Stanford started to get up but Sam pulled him back, holding him.

"Stay," Sam said softly.

And Stanford did. His lover was the only person who could truly soothe him. Stanford often felt bewitched, as if Sam's careless but genuine love for life had snaked under his skin. He leaned into Sam, who always smelled of lilac.

"You sounded angry," Sam said. "Were you angry?"

"At her? How could I be?" Stanford said.

For the first few months after she died, he had dreamed of her, and began to hope she would haunt him. But she never did. And the dreams disappeared.

"She saved Bo's life," Stanford said. "She insisted I go to the lake. It was her. Not me."

For a moment, Stanford saw Granny Emma's bold eyes, her smiling face. Stanford tried to recall the earlier dreams of her, those that had haunted him right after her death. But they were only tattered fragments.

"It doesn't make any sense," Stanford said.

"We all have nightmares," Sam said, taking his hand.

Stanford kept his eyes closed and waited for sleep, wanting it to come swiftly, hoping for some absolute blackness, but as he fell there was a familiar rustling of leaves in the wind and deeper still, her voice. He had not heard it in such a long time, and now, sweaty and dream beaten, he did not want to remember her warning in the kitchen, he wanted to squash the memory like pulp in his hand because thinking of her hurt. He pulled Sam close, burying his face in his lover's back. It was there that he dissolved into sleep.

26

Richard, Brownsville, 1951

The land stretched out flat and wild. There was rich honey-tipped grass, a thrust of country fluttering, cawing, scattering. Richard stood, while Emma nestled at his feet.

"What's over that hill?" she said.

In the distance, the acres sloped steadily upward to an unseen horizon.

"A nice lake," Richard said.

She reached out and held onto his lower leg, then leaned into him. He stayed stiff thinking of the country home he would build for them to retire to, seeing it all in front of him, the color and grain of the wood, the logs harnessed from not far off.

"Will it bother you, him being so close?" Emma said.

Ricard sighed. He knew what she meant, and over the years, in seeing things come to be, he did not immediately reject what she said. Still, he couldn't give in so easily to her witchery, despite the fact that the minute they parked their pick up and wandered across the acres, he felt the presence of his brother Rolf.

"The camp was a few miles from here," he said.

Emma squeezed his leg.

"The dead hover high up. Being present is different for

them," she said. "He's with us, and he will be close if we settle here."

There came then a strong summer wind, and the high golden-tipped grass bent fast, and Richard knew Rolf was indeed near, and that the grass bending was his touching the earth, the same earth that grew the tree that killed him. He knew Emma was right.

"Where do you want the summer kitchen?" he said.

On this she stood, leaning closer, pointing to the spot for the kitchen, then wrapping her hands around his waist.

"Are you ready to sell the Allemania Street house to make this home?" she said.

"Cal is grown and settled," he said. "Can we be happy here?"

He was asking himself as much as her, knowing this step forward was in many ways a return, a collapsing back into a long-ago forgotten dream, a long-ago abandoned grief that if it weren't for Emma surely would have killed him.

"I can be happy anywhere with you," she said.

The wind tossed the grass around some more, and he turned and lifted her up easily and gently, carrying her in his arms across the land, up the hill to the peak with its view of the lake, and its gentle glimpse of a past not forgotten.

27

Cal, St. Louis, 1970

The earth was deep red and wet. It was plowed clean and smooth, a sharply squared-off empty lot bordered by manicured lawns and neighbors' homes. Cal brought a lawn chair for himself and his son, who would arrive soon.

He watched the sky abandon all color as the sun set quickly. He gripped the sides of the chair thinking that if he stood up fast and did something he could halt that dying light, that end of day, he could get his breath and make sense of things. But a jagged slice of moon was already there, and the night had come without his consent.

He had built the house that had filled this plot and he now recalled the rooms, still hovering there mirage-like, and too the additions to the house after his son was born, the sewing nook Josie had wanted. He saw those rooms rise up, the walls that changed colors every few years, those first striped wool curtains she'd made herself that hung too long. And now he had torn it all down. Nothing left. Cal rubbed his forehead and reached for a beer in the small cooler near his chair. He had to explain this all to his son before Stanford went back to university in New York in the morning. He did not know what to say; still, something had to be said.

The dark crept in, the plot now lit partially by neighbors'

porch lights, and he tried to see her there, washing dishes or reading a book, but he saw nothing. He could hear Stanford's Mustang approaching. He heard the motor go off, the door swing and slam shut, then footsteps.

"Hey Dad," Stanford said. "Beer? That's not like you."

He sat next to his father and opened a can.

"I used to drink beer and play cards during the war," Cal said. "Scotch came later."

"Ok," Stanford said.

He wanted to get right into it, why he'd torn down the house that year while Stanford was at school, how he felt about Josie, his increasing sense of urgency to get life back in order. But these words did not come.

"How's school?" Cal said.

"Good. Bo and I bought another condemned building, you know like we did last summer," Stanford said. "The market is good. We've been making some decent money."

"What?" Cal said.

He turned to look at his son, who was tall, lean and tanned, wearing all white. Then, feeling restless, he got up and walked across the damp plot of land, entering phantom rooms, all gone, imagining scents and tables crowded with things, ideas, plans. He suddenly could not recall his son's age, did not understand his talk of buying buildings and making money, and this momentarily devastated him, for they were there to talk about the future and what had happened and he wanted to be in charge of this but he felt very lost. Stanford got up and followed him. They stood in the center of the empty lot that once was their family home. He couldn't remember the last time he'd had a conversation with his son. Stanford was looking at him with concern, as if he were already too far gone, as if he were absolutely lost.

"I couldn't stand it here without her," Cal said. "I had to tear it all down."

"It's ok, Dad," Stanford said softly.

Cal turned and looking at his son, knew what it was he actually needed to say, knew there was something other than his own grief and anger.

"Don't let things go so easily," Cal said. "Focus on the things you have. What's in front of you. Don't ignore things. I want you to understand that. I want you to."

For a moment Cal thought he heard a voice and he spun around, stepping away and listening, for it was a soft voice and it was close to him. The land in front of him appeared suddenly vast, empty of any structure, and he regretted ripping down the house, that memory, and he saw in the vast, endless night entirely what he had lost and this was too much.

He fell into the dirt and dug his hands, then started to grab and claw at the wet earth, yanking clumps and tossing them aside, pushing his hands further and deeper as if he would discover a new frontier. He pushed at the dirt with his muscles even when he felt a hand on his shoulder, when he heard a small gentle voice coax him up. His body quaked and he could not stand on his own, taken in now by such huge and irreparable damage. He let his son guide him away from the hole, the red dirt, the home, to the black Mustang. And neither of them looked back as they drove away, and neither of them spoke. They let the night's blackness fill that void.

28

Stanford, Zambia, 1992

Stanford and Bo were free-wheeling in a jeep, not far from their camp, armed and tired, lolling across the African plains. They were near the end of an elaborate four-day hunting trip. Bo had set up the adventure back in Manhattan, when a new and very important client had confessed over a late-night scotch that a safari was on his bucket list. The scheme had worked. They sealed a multi-million-dollar real estate deal that day. Their final hunt was later that evening, and they would all fly back to New York in the morning.

The jeep leapt up over a small incline and Stanford and Bo saw the water buffalo.

Before them, there was a slow devouring taking place on a sunburnt grassy plain. The animal was lying on its side, huge curled antlers and eyes searching heaven, its skin grey-black, smudged paler in spots, with a gash sliced clean in its center as its insides leaked. The bovine began to moan, a long low and deep howling of death and defeat.

"That's incredible," said Bo.

There were three lions near the dying beast, and one holding the water buffalo in its grasp, tongue wagging, waiting for it to give up completely. Stanford knew that they had missed the fight, but surely the group of lions had surrounded the larger beast and overpowered it.

"We best go," Bo said. "Before they notice us. They can run as fast as this jeep and I'm a terrible shot."

Stanford gripped the steering wheel, waiting for one last moment, as if something was going to happen he needed to see. The dying beast slowly turned its head, its jaw opening up as its eyes flared wide, wider then seemed possible, staring straight at Stanford.

He floored the jeep and spun the wheel, tearing back to the camp. Bo turned to watch their dust.

"Nothing followed. The lions seem happy with what they got," Bo said.

As evening swept in with an assured force, Bo began to sing and Stanford tried to discard the grotesque vision, but he could not. He was unable to forget the terrible look the animal had given him, as if those eyes held some divinity, not just the terror of a dying soul.

Men hunched with guns shouldered on bench rests, aimed into the oblivion of a sweltering African night. Stanford drew a ragged breath. He felt deeply unsettled.

His Ruger safari rifle, butt pressed to his shoulder, weighed over a hundred pounds. The gun's large caliber cartridge (a .577 tyrannosaur) had a ferocious kick back. He'd seen a two-hundred pound man reel onto his ass after squeezing the trigger.

There were five other men huddled on an incline facing

a wide expanse of rock-strewn earth. These hunters were hired locals armed and ready to shoot. Then there was Bo, who sat on the sidelines drinking. Bo was not a hunter. He'd come along only for the brief but very important business portion of the journey. The client for whom the whole trip was planned had left that afternoon, due to an unexpected banking emergency. So much planning had gone into the final night's expedition that they went forward with it anyway.

The night sky was endlessly black. One of the locals snapped on a narrow spotlight bolder than the moon. A jackal froze, a framed image shattered by one shot. The animal snapped electrically, its body popping inward, falling dead. The light snapped off.

"We're hunting leopards, not jackals," Stanford said. "Don't shoot at just anything. And keep that light off."

The deep stillness had been disrupted by the hapless shooter. The group settled in to wait for its prey. Not so far off a meek howling began. The residual pixilating burn of the electric light faded and Stanford's eyes adjusted again to the black. Grass bristled. Soft, rushing things murmured.

Stanford scanned the darkness. If a leopard didn't come along soon he'd call it a night. Bo had been up and down several times, to take a leak, to once howl at the moon before Stanford shut him up. Suddenly, from a distance, came a terrible screaming.

"What is that?" Stanford said.

Sitting next to him was Zad, the local high priest and paid listener, a man who could hear a leopard move from a mile off. Zad could also see a leopard in the deep darkness before any other human eye, they said.

"The black leopard holds within its heart the souls of a

thousand dead tribesmen," Zad said. "She is near."

Stanford thought of what was about to happen, the killing of the leopard, and he shuddered with a swift and sudden fear. He tried to stand, but Zad pushed him back down.

"She is here," Zad whispered.

Stanford saw nothing but heard that constant and terrible distant screaming and felt Zad's strong grip, his hot breath, whispering something in another tongue, guiding Stanford's hand, his finger on the trigger, as if he saw the golden eye of the beast, the slow voluptuous movement slinking forward to devour them all until there it was, without thinking, moving finger over bone-smooth trigger. The money shot. His shot, then four more shots from the other hunters to assure the job was done. Then the quiet.

"She is dead," Zad said softly.

"All right," Stanford said.

There was soft applause. The spotlights snapped on. The leopard lay felled and graceful, fully stretched limbs and sleek head settled on the earth in repose. In the wide arc of the light, stretching out of frame, lay something else far to the right of the native scene. The applause stopped.

It was Bo in the brush, near the earlier felled jackal. His head had been blown off.

29

Cal, Missouri, 1990

On November 24, Cal collapsed onto the raked and vacant plot of land that had held his family home, that back porch, nursery-turned-boy's-room and sturdy kitchen table where he once made love to his wife Josie. He had never had the heart to sell the land, after demolishing the house years back. A lone mighty oak tree had been left standing.

A neighbor, Mrs. Beatty Driscoll, discovered Cal lying near the oak. He was face up in the rich red earth, eyes open and lips parted as if mid-sentence, telling some cruel truth to the morning sky. Mrs. Driscoll said he looked older than she remembered him.

Everything Cal had, that plot of land, the lumber mill, and the acreage known as Rolf's retreat, went to his only son, Stanford.

30

Stanford, New York, 1992

For their one-year anniversary, Stanford surprised Sam by hiring a car to take them to a dazzling little restaurant on a bluff overlooking the upper Hudson River Valley. He rented the place for the night, and sent detailed instructions regarding how the table should be set, what wines should be served, the menu and the timing for an opera singer to perform. He planned to propose to Sam, and brought an 18k rose gold Tiffany ring with pavé diamonds. They sat outside at a bluff-side table at dusk. In the slow dying light, the river below appeared a milky blue, then silver, then darker. Across the river, the facing bluffs rose with their imperfect and jagged beauty, and there was a brilliant blood red shade to the sky.

Sam was staring at an oyster.

"You don't have to eat it," Stanford said.

"I don't think I can," Sam said.

There were oval-shaped electric lights, shaded with colored paper, strung on wire and lining the edges of the restaurant. A very lean, flat-chested young woman with white hair in a shimmering gold dress played a harp in a far corner. The lamps shivered on and off before settling into a soft glow. Very slowly, as they drank their first bottle of wine, constellations etched outlines on the night sky.

"You amaze me, Stanford," Sam said. "I mean really. Boy, you just never stop surprising me."

From their first meeting, Stanford had always surprised Sam with gifts (clothes, shoes, paintings, a small white dog, a piano) but this was the first time he took him out of the city.

There was a second wine, and Sam confessed that he liked the trout caviar, and the cheeses and even the faux gras.

"I'm just a louse," Sam said.

"What is that? A bird?"

"A louse? It's like a dumb ass. I read that paper is for a one-year anniversary, so I ordered paper whites, the fancy flowers, and they won't arrive until next week, so I've got nothing to give you."

"I like doing things for you," Stanford said.

There was a commotion over the river, the sound of birds cawing. Stanford could see a wide wingspan, flying near the top of the cliff, turning in an arc then diving down toward the water. He couldn't make out what kind of bird it was. He stood up to watch it soar. The bird skimmed the water and scooped something up. And in that moment, as he sat back down, as the waiter set down simmered venison, as the harpist moved her hands more swiftly to her song's conclusion, he thought of Bo.

It had been six months since Bo had died in Africa. He looked across at Sam and there was silence. The harp stopped. The opera singer was beginning a selection from Faust. Stanford kept his eyes on Sam. He did not want to look back at the river, did not want to see flailing things, did not want to realize what lurked there. The river had unexpectedly stirred him and he did not like that. He needed to focus. He took Sam's hand.

"Stanford, what's wrong?" Sam said.

"Nothing," Stanford said.

Stanford's hand was trembling. He had prepared a speech. The opera singer roared. The song was not right. He could not think. He'd had it all planned so perfectly. The man's voice was overwhelming, beastly, and he wanted to scream at him to shut up, to let him think, and he cursed Bo, cursed that water-born memory of his first, perhaps purest love who was devouring this moment, and he felt a deep, deep running grief and he thought too of his dead father.

"Stanford tell me what's wrong," Sam said.

The singer kept on and the moment was ruined. Sam squeezed his hand.

"I was thinking of Bo," Stanford said, lowering his eyes. "I don't know why. I'm sorry."

"It's only been six months. It was a terrible thing," Sam said. "Don't apologize, I know how much you loved him."

And with that the singer finished his first selection and Stanford heard a horrible rustling in the dark and he shut his eyes thinking, *What have I done?*

"I blame myself," Stanford said softly.

"It was an accident," Sam said. "Don't do that."

At that Sam got up and went to Stanford's side and brought Stanford's head to his chest and cradled him there and Stanford thought, *He does not know, this boy does not know,* and he wanted to tell him about the dreams he'd been having, of Bo in pieces, of his Granny Emma far in the distance yelling at him and him not hearing her, ignoring her warnings, but instead he reached in his coat pocket and drew out the ring and took Sam's hand and put the ring in his palm.

"I fucked this up," Stanford said.

Sam opened his palm and gasped as the opera singer began again, more gently this time, and the waiters lingered in shadows, uncertain and amused.

"It's perfect," Sam said. "I love you, Stanford."

And with that Stanford let himself fall deeply, more deeply then he thought possible, into his bright young lover's embrace.

31

Stanford rose through the warm lake water, which was murky until he reached that gentle, clear breaking point at the surface. As a swimmer, Stanford had always enjoyed this gradual emerging, diving deep then rising with precision, slowly moving from muted to bright, as if meeting a new world each time.

He paused at the top near that watery skin, opening his eyes wide. He could hold his breath a very long time. He heard distant laughter and shouting. Finally, he shot up spear-like, tossing watery residue off of his head, surfacing into the heat of morning.

In the distance, his mother sat stiffly on the grassy shore, her shoulders arched, steel silvery head held high, her feet primly tucked under, not moving, like an animal caught in a sudden beam of light. She looked strange and intense, out of place on the grass, as if she would bolt any minute. He thought of an article he had recently read. It was about a nomadic species that never settled in one place, and devoured the weakest of their young if they could not keep pace. Was it sea turtles in Galapagos?

Beyond her were a few stray fruit trees, then the road up to the house and the summer kitchen, then a bluebird swooping down, and it seemed too that there was a man, a specter waving to him. But that vanished as he wiped his eyes again, treading water.

There was a shriek and he turned to see Sam and their little son Bo on the floating dock, jumping foot to foot, then raising their arms over their heads in some sort of tribal dance. Bo could not quite keep up with Sam so they kept starting over, and their laughter was boisterous as their movements became increasingly chaotic. Finally, they stood side by side at the dock's edge and lifted their arms slowly in unison, over their heads in a V. Sam towered over Bo, both of them dressed in cotton trunks decorated with monkeys swinging from vines. In an instant, they were airborne, splashing into the lake.

Stanford turned back to shore where his mother sat watching. He swam in and went to her.

"Do not shake water on me," Josie said.

Stanford shrugged. She was dressed for a cocktail party. Her silver hair was swept back in an elegant coif, and she wore a silk scarf around her neck, a soft green cotton dress and bone-white leather sandals.

"Are you wearing false eye lashes?" he asked, glancing at her, sitting gingerly on the edge of her checked blanket.

Between them was a basket Josie had packed. Three cheeses, fruits, wine and sparkling water for Bo, who at seven already had begun to develop an appetite for things as rare as oysters, plums and figs, thanks to his Grandmother Josie.

Josie ignored her son's question, and pulled out two glasses.

"Is it too early for wine?" she said.

She poured the wine and they both drank, watching the

lake. There was a long silence but Stanford did not try to fill it. The shore had a slight incline. He was sitting just behind and to the side of his mother so he saw her in profile. She was rigid. Everything about her was sharp—the angles of her face, her fiercely manicured brows, the bold swoop of her sprayed hair. She looked anxious and ready to spring and Stanford noticed a slight trembling of her chin.

"Are you all right?" he finally said.

Josie turned her head, though only slightly. She did not look at Stanford.

"I was thinking of your grandmother. We used to picnic here. I never liked the out of doors."

"Granny Emma?"

"Yes."

There was another stretch of silence, and Stanford realized that while their relationship had softened over the last few years thanks to her more regular visits from Paris, he still held simmering resentments, which came out when they were together. He refused to exchange pleasant conversation with his mother and as a rule, they did not spend much time alone together.

"It's funny," she said.

"What."

"She knew I was pregnant with you before I did," she said.

"Well, she had that gift," he said.

Sam and Bo appeared back up on the floating dock. One mighty cloud momentarily eclipsed the sun and everything was thrust into shadow, the lake darkening to a harder green. Stanford recalled the times he'd swam here, and of his boyhood, but he tried to shove those memories away. He did not like to think of that past, or of Bo or his grandma, but then here it was, crawling up, taking him under for a moment.

"We were sitting right here when she told me," she said.

"What did she say?" he said.

"Don't be afraid, you're going to be a good mother," Josie said.

"That's it?"

Josie rose up on her knees, turning slowly and repositioning herself on the blanket, facing Stanford.

"I had not done much of anything in my life," she said. "I did what my father told me. Then I did what your father told me. I guess she was trying to help me. I was so unsure of everything."

On the dock, Sam and Bo had lain down, side by side.

"You were sitting here alone with her?" Stanford said.

"Yes," Josie said. "When she told me that, I didn't know if I was really pregnant or even what I thought about being pregnant, but she had that look, and she took my hands. She was a strange woman. She frightened me."

Stanford turned away from her, looking up the hill toward the house and the summer kitchen. It was all so still. He remembered being frightened by Granny Emma too.

"She said things to me like that," Stanford said. "And gave me things."

He did not look at his mother, rather kept his eyes on the top of the hill and his memory of what lay beyond, wishing that Granny Emma would appear there, ghostly white from head to toe as if dunked in cake flour, spry and tiny, coming back to remind them of her powers.

"What did she give you?" Josie said.

Stanford turned back to his mother and she was smiling, leaning back on one arm. He tried to imagine her all those years ago at twenty sitting here with Granny Emma, then he tried to recall what Granny Emma had given him, but all he could think of was the plum cake she made, and blowing out candles with his new friend Bo at his side. She had sent him to the lake to find Bo. She had told him other things. She had warned him. She had given him a chance to change the future, but he had ignored her, forgotten her. What exactly was it she had said in the summer kitchen? It was all buried so deeply.

"Why didn't you come here for my twelfth birthday?" he said.

At this Josie turned away from him, looking out to the lake.

"I was angry at your father. That wasn't fair to you was it?" she said.

"You were always angry at him."

"Not at the beginning, no," she said.

A bird with a massive wingspan swung high above them, cawing very loudly. Josie jumped and screamed at the sound. Then she began to laugh. He watched her as she laughed harder, not a lady's laugh, then finally she lay back on the blanket and covered her mouth with her hand. He noticed her fingernails were painted pink, something he had not noticed before.

"Or maybe I was always angry; I just didn't know how to handle that," she said. "Oh God that poor fox."

"What fox?"

Josie kept her hand on her face. The sun was bright.

"Your father never told you?" she said.

"No."

"You were in your crib. On the porch. It was so hot."

'How old was I?" Stanford said.

He sat up on his knees, oddly excited. They did not talk about the past. In his mind, his thoughts of his mother always began the year she left them.

"You were a year old," she said. "I swear it was 108 and your father wanted to sit on the porch. A fox wandered over from the fields. Back then, there wasn't much around. I was so hot and mad at your father and at you."

"Me?"

At this she sat up again. She looked out at the lake.

"You have a child now," she said. "It changes things."

He never imagined his mother being angry at him; he gave so much energy to his being angry at her. He never thought much of his impact on her. He watched her watching his son, and he thought too of Granny Emma watching him, speaking to him, and he knew there were terrible regrets, misty things hovering just above the surface of his life, things he knew, thought of sometimes just as he was falling asleep, dreamed of and forgot, and he knew too it was what she had told him long ago that really haunted him. And Bo. Granny Emma had said it was just the root of things. The flaws of being human. Wasn't that it?

"It all goes by so quickly," Josie said. "We do our best."

She lowered her head and to him, she looked very frail. Stanford stood up.

"Let's go up. We can make lunch," he said.

She turned to him, and he reached out his hand and he helped her up. And together, they went to the summer kitchen.

32

Richard, Brownsville, 1970

They were at the lake and the lake was still. Richard held a letter in his hand. A dozen dragonflies circled in magic patterns just above them and Emma pointed and clapped her hands at the beauty of their dance.

Richard sighed and put the letter into his pocket.

"I don't understand why this happened," Richard said. "Help me understand, Emma."

She took his hand, kissed it, then opened his palm touching one long thin line that skirted from mid palm to wrist.

"It's right here dear, the root of everything," Emma said.

A second swarm of dragonflies joined the group, now hovering closer to the lake's edge, as the water slowly lost its glimmer and the summer sun fell away toward dusk and a lion's moon.

'Don't give me riddles," he said.

She smiled and squeezed his hand.

"*Sosa I cad Ta Tu* is the Celtic. Rest in what you are," Emma said. "That's what my granny said year after year. That is what she stitched into her quilts and into our lives. That is the root of everything. "

Richard sighed.

"*Er ist verioren*," he said softly.

Richard had taught Emma some German through the years as she had taught him some Celtic. When he was upset he spoke his native tongue.

"Cal is not lost," Emma said.

"His wife left him" he said. "His son moved across the country. All we have is a few lines on paper. He won't come see us. He doesn't talk to me. I have failed him just as I failed my brother Rolf."

Richard pulled his hand away and covered his face, and with this sharp action, the dragonflies scattered as if this human grief had poisoned their air.

"No," she said.

"I have failed them both. My brother and now my son."

"What did his letter say?" Emma said.

"Not a lot," Richard said. "He blames himself. He tore down their home. Why won't he come see us, Emma?"

"He will," she said.

He lowered his head, looking down at the earth as if it held some answer, and the dragonflies moved toward them again, hovering in a wide circle. Emma took his hand and kissed the tips of his fingers, then pointed to the oldest, mightiest tree on their land.

"Look there," she said. "Our tree has seen so much and survived."

Indeed the oak was massive, a monster of a tree. It had withstood two tornadoes and so many years and now ruled the landscape of scattered elms and spruces. There was one huge branch, near the bottom of the tree where all the limbs began to split off from the center, which had been partially severed when lightning struck it. The huge branch was torn open in just one spot, revealing its meaty white bark. But the cut had not killed it; rather the hefty branch forged westerly, growing out farther than any of the tree's limbs.

"It is so strong," Emma said, standing and pointing.

As she did a flock of black birds swept over the lake toward the oak, this movement stirring the dragonflies, which scattered, also moving toward the distant line of trees. The insects quickly disappeared from view, though the birds, flying in a V, could be seen for quite a while, until they made a sharp turn. And were gone.

"Cal will find his way, same as you found your way," Emma said.

"But I didn't find my way, I found you," Richard said.

"Or did I find you?" she said.

"Yes you did," Richard said.

She sat again at his side. As evening came, and a pale moon graced the lake, she pulled out from a large pocket in her gingham smock a paperweight.

"I have been saving this for a long time," she said, putting the flat glass paperweight in his hand. "I bought it at the St. Louis Fair."

Richard held it in his palm and it was cool against his skin. Inside the slender glass was an image of the famed Ferris Wheel. Below the wheel was listed in faded ink its height of 264 feet and its weight of 4300 tons.

"Rolf would have loved to ride on that," Richard said.

"Yes," said Emma.

He closed his hand over the glass.

"I miss him still, Emma," he said.

"Rolf would have soared on that big wheel," Emma said, pointing to the night sky. "And he soars above us now."

And with that, Richard's grief, which had for so long been tortured and gnarled, hard and angry, turned soft as falling snow, and he leaned into his love, and gently cried, giving himself to her, hearing only the sound of a new wind, and his brother's long ago voice calling to him to slow down as they climbed that hill in the wilds of Brownsville, rising toward the peak looking down on the lumber camp, not knowing then what lay beyond.

Lightning

Fayetteville, Arkansas
1918

1

"Boy birthed big," Gran said. "Flew off yonder table, slick greased'n wild eyed."

Gran was the family spinner. Ice cold winter nights, in the hard shadow of our wood stove, me and her'd hunch down soft and close like hunters. Her eyes'd fire up, and she'd tell it to me so it was happening right then.

"You swoops out Boy like your'n bird and I holler he's fixing to fly," Gran whispered, wind rattling the walls of the house, Ma and Pa long asleep. "Lightning, call him Lightning."

That was her best spin, my birth. They didn't call me Lightning, though, called me Bud after Pa's dead brother. Fact is they don't call me Bud neither. Call me Boy. Seems like Gran cursed or blessed my birth naming, depends on how you look on it. Nothing stuck to me but Boy. I loved Gran something awful, so it was hard when she died short after I turned twelve. Glad I got to know her that long.

Gran was strong and fast up to her last breath. Wild fast, like spit-flash never ceasing, emptying Pa's tobacco tin, dancing out to the coops at sun up, plucking a squash to gut mash for soup, hauling Peepaw in after his worst shit drinking. She was something.

The last day for her, that was bad. That death day I can't never forget. Wild coon dog dragged Gran by one stiffed up

131

crack-thin arm, yanking her from the root garden out back, pulling her near the well. That devil dog barked, pressed his face on mutt paws, let his eyes roam yonder to see who might be watching. I'd come out from morning chores, standing dumb and slow on the porch watching the whole thing. It took me time to figure it out. Then I started running. I raised both hands and squawked while that mutt went down for a slow gnaw on the handful of okra Gran had a death-grip on. The dog couldn't get at the greens, so he started chomping at her clamped knuckles, bloodied them, until I kicked him hard. Dog yelped and ran and Gran looked right at me, eyes wide, like a spin was gonna bubble up from her gap-open mouth and tell me straight how I done swooped outa my momma. How they shoulda called me Lightning. How she loved me best.

It was my first gawk at death. I wasn't ghost scared but hot all over. Like my insides was boiling and my heart was splitting. Gran always said I was the riled type. That was truth. Lots of things riled me something awful: like crossing the field behind our house at night; or them wild death dances of lost chickens headless chasing scrappy feed; or the taste when I'd push my tongue all secret-like to the inside of the winter barn door, that musty bitter ring in my mouth viper sweet.

Looking at Gran that day, I was hot and aching, but not scared. Truth was, I woulda sunk and cried and wailed and beat things up for a dern long spell after she died, but that was the same season the horse came. It wasn't that I forgot Gran, she was just smothered by something bigger.

Of course, I called him Lightning.

2

Pa won the "damn ugly animal" playing poker. Cards, he swore, was the only right way to get on with life's "natty ass messes" like Gran's death. He'd said the day after he won the animal, all red eyed, gut stinky and angry, that he'd almost grabbed the jar of Whittley's moonshine over the beast, but at the last second he'd said, "Gimme the horse."

He'd been fired up and fixed on riding it home through the ice-spitting rain from the Whittley's farm. Pa's a scant man. That night he'd forgot his shoes and ended up barefoot. Lightweight or not, the horse had shucked his skinny frame off like the lid off a fizzed pop bottle. Pa had sailed into the weeds and cussed at the thing before getting back up on it. Next morning, Pa swore the beast off and told me straight.

"Take care of dat damn thing. I ain't aimin' ta see it."

First chance I had to meet the horse came round twilight. A fat-lick of day chores were done, Baby Sis put to sleep, food gone and plates cleaned. Ma and Pa were shut away night-huddling. It was dark as I made my way out to see the animal, smiling and thinking *it's mine*. I'd been dreaming about having my own horse since I was ten, when I read about the fearsome bandit Billy the Kid who could ride faster than an arrow could fly. My best friend Jerky Peck had his own horse for three years already and I was plum jealous. Jerky could fly across a field and hop over a hedge like nobody's business and he was even learning to work a rope.

Making my way real quiet through the cold night, I imagined Billy riding up from the woods. I wished I coulda met him. I hid a newspaper picture of him in my cigar box, along with a blue bird feather and a smooth black stone Gran gave me. Late some nights I'd stare real close at that picture, trying to figure out what he was thinking with that crazy shit-eating grin, puffing his chest out, hitching his hands deep into his pant waist. I dreamed once that he and I wrestled, rolling over and over across a dusty hot desert, neither of us winning.

I had a secret plan to move out west with Jerky and live the wild life of a cowboy. I knew not to breathe a word of that, since Pa would wallop me into next week for having such a "damn dumb ass idea." Thing was, Pa didn't like if anybody did anything or thought anything better than he did. He liked to come up with most every idea. Maybe if I learned to ride real well, it might cross Pa's mind that I'd make a first-rate cowboy.

The barn sat a good spell away from the house, built that way cause Pa said he didn't want to be "smelling no mule shit whiles I sleep off a good one." In winter I cussed him, since it was so dern cold and the wide black field I had to cross gave me the heart shivers. Weird things rustled out there. I never said nothing to nobody, but something was in that high grass, down the ravine past gnarled and storm-chewed trees. Shredded deadwood leaked black goo and wrinkled up like lightning scarred devils. Soft rustling things, hell maybe even Gran's ghost. If it'd been up to me, I woulda built the barn close to the house, mule shit or no.

Through the field, in the dark, the barn always snuck

up. It was blackish so it didn't announce itself. The doors were heavy and oily, smeared with mud and splattered with messes of junk. It always took a good heave for me to open them. At the barn door I felt the circling new ache in my lower belly, and that jittery need to secret-kiss the soft wood door or even lick into a splinter. That queer yearning came up, but I stopped as the animal neighed from inside.

The sound was like a touch, a soft hand come to my face, but a touch kinda inside and under my skin, both mean like Pa and weak like my scaredness. The closeness of the noise shook me. It hit me so I sat right down in the dirt under a flaming yellow moon. I waited and listened cause it was like the animal inside knew I was sitting with my shivering knees pulled chin-close at the foot of the barn door.

It was bone-still and past the twilling tree frogs was the thick breath of the thing, pressing air in and out of its horsey nostrils. Ass on the cold earth, I'd got my foot pressed against the barn door, almost afraid to push it open to get a peek at it. I breathed deep and listened to the animal's nose sound, matching it breath for breath. The sucking got me dizzy. I felt like the horse had busted from his stall, like he had come closer toward the barn door from the other side like a thin shadow. The sound of his breath was shutting out the night. My damn short leg couldn't reach to get the door open any more and the night air tickled my ankle. It was like he had nuzzled there, like his face got hot near me, like any second I woulda felt the breath, the wet horse tongue on my leg.

I jumped up and pushed into the barn and the animal stared all cool from the stall, lolling his meaty tongue over wide flat teeth. We both shuddered, discovering the other: he all bold and strong, me scrawny for my age, just over five foot and ninety-five pounds wet. I went and opened the stall and drew at him and he leaned his face down toward me, holding still, the touching scent. I was afraid but reached out because there was Gran's voice close saying, "Lightning." He sniffed at me, then threw his head back and snorted. He gave me a good long stare and I reached out my hand for him to sniff.

Moving real slow, I touched the animal's bruised and bitten-on face and he didn't seem to mind, which surprised me. He was a gentle, good looking horse, a rich brown color with a tar black mane. I ran my hand back and forth along his soft, warm flank and felt him shudder a little as he turned his head to get a side-eyed look at me. I slowly pressed a finger over and inside hot cove nostrils then down to the wet mouth and eased a finger up there real quick, feeling a harshness of teeth and a strength. He snapped his head away and I figured I was lucky he didn't bite me. I ran my hand along his flank again, gently back and forth, and then I pressed my cheek on his side and whispered to him, "All right, it's all right." We stayed like that, like a couple dancing and I felt him lean into me and I thought *he's lonesome*, then I heard again "Lightning" like that black field grass was coming alive and getting at us both.

"I'm Bud," I said, face on the animal's side. "Hey there Lightning."

That was the start.

3

I shared a room with Bonnie May, who we all called Baby Sis. We was in the back of the house and there was a wide window looking out toward the dark mess of that creepy black field leading to the barn. My bed was pushed against the window so I looked out at night sometimes, before I fell off to sleep.

Pa and Uncle Bud done built our house with "their own hands and sweat and some kinda miracle," Ma said. The men worked until their "bones near busted in half." The building money came from Ma's fancy rich sister Gert, who lived out east in New York City. The summer they built it, they got help from Mr. Whittley and the Potter brothers. Pa said Whittley and the Potters started showing up just to watch, then help, then celebrate with moonshine under a soft summer moon.

"It was a good un, that summer," Pa said. "Them was good times, then."

Ways back, before they up and died, Pa's folks Gran and Peepaw owned the land outright and everybody lived in a saggy little cabin until Ma started blooming with me, her first. The money from Gert stoked a hot light of something fresh in Pa, and the building of the farm started and finished all in that one long summer. Uncle Bud woulda had the room Bonnie May and I was in, but Bud went off to work west, Pa said, and two years later, he died. Pa wouldn't talk about how Bud went. Nothing much really got said of Bud's leaving or how that end came.

Staring out back at the field, I was half asleep but could see a soft blur coming through the grass. The thing coming forward probably had the mouth of a tractor and jaws to snap me and Sis in half. But the clear moon quieted that ghost, and the face crept closer against night and I could see the horse's eyes like some violet vision in the dark. Lightning came to the window, seeking me, lonely out there in the cold and I cussed soft thinking how I musta left the barn door open, and thinking if Pa woke up I'd be in for it. I got dressed in a hurry and went out. The house was still, so I was safe.

"What you doing Lightning?" I said. "You can't come in the house."

He tossed his head back against the clear black night sky and I figured he liked that idea. I led him back to the barn, but stopped at the door. I sucked my fingers to warm them. I had a sudden bad urge to get up on him. I'd ridden a mule and a plow horse a few times, but hadn't never done any riding just to ride. And never on my own horse. I sometimes rode on the back of Jerky's horse with him, but that was different.

"Night riding. Climb on up there Boy," Gran's voice said.

I'd heard Gran's voice pretty much regular since she'd passed and was glad for it. Standing, staring at Lightning, the cold made my lips feel raw and dry and I thought of Gran and of heat. I thought back to how they'd burnt Gran, and that hurting fire. Pa always said land was too precious to waste on dead graves. His kin, the Tilleys, always put their dead to rest in fire. Tradition. The day of Gran's burning, it all went quick. Sizzle, crack, pop, nasty sounds. The bones crushed and snapping. Lots of big trees sacrificed for that pyre. It made me think of burning witches, but I done kept that to myself.

"She good well gone to glory," Pa had said.

I watched the whole burning that day cause I didn't want to lose any last snap second of Gran, even if it meant her melting in the fire, her skinny soft wrist crackling to naked bone while leaves flew into her hair and fire flamed and popped up through her eyes, brains, glory. I watched that burning like religion was on me, watched it to the bitterest flaming end. Pa buried the bones out in the back field once it was done, this all part of the Tilley family ritual that his kin had passed on for years, like a dark hot blessing.

"Clean 'er up with fire, that good soul," Pa had said, looking away, not meeting anybody's eyes that day.

So when Gran's voice came at me soon after, a few words at a time in my head, or sometimes rising up like a violent bile echo in my scrawny throat, I was surely happy. She was around whispering during times like this, when I faced up to gut things that I knew scarce nothing about.

"Climb up, grab on," Gran's voice said.

I stomped and huffed a bit, pounding my fists together, thinking for a second that I was the horse, and my footwork shooed Lightning away from the barn door. He trotted straight into the field, that place that was all terror at night. Creeps. Dead things. The ghost of Billy the Kid waiting to grab me. Lightning skittered out there fast, like nothing could harm us, and I followed.

It was mighty cold and the sky was flat and black. We stood and stared at one another in the moonlight. I put my hand on his flank, ran it down to his rump and back to his mane. I couldn't get my eyes away from the horse eyes, so big and wild on his mighty head. They didn't stare right at you, they crept along the side of the big beastly face, spilling open unto you like some silky cotton shoved in a socket and licked with night-oil. Those eyes were wet and waiting and I swore he was nudging me to ride him. Facing the wind, we waited together as if something was going to happen.

I felt tiny in that wide crawling field of night under the inky sky. Felt like a fleck of dust. I was shivering something awful.

"Go on," Gran's voice said.

Truth was, I feared Lightning could be gone soon. Pa was already scraping around all snarly, saying, "We ain't got none to feed that damn varmint. Shit I shoulda took me the moonshine. My brains like a bug's ass." Ma laughed at that one.

Standing in the ice cold now, eyes locked with Lightning, I hoped Pa didn't get no crazy notion to cook him some horse steak. I needed to find a way to put Lightning to good use.

"Climb up," Gran's voice said again.

I took a step forward and he tapped one hoof down, pressing the crow-black earth. I stepped even closer, aching a little now in the night's shivery bitterness. I touched him on the crest and was getting ready to hoist myself up when he made an awful noise. Lightning reared his big head back and whinnied, tossing that dark mane back and forth. I pressed a hand on his side and petted slowly. He settled, lowered his head, and turned to one side so one big eye saw mine.

"Gonna ride ya Lightning," I said. "You and me."

Lightning let his eyes waver, then turned down low, lolling a little. He blew out air like he was ready, but I had to get that horse down, or get myself up there. My head just about reached the saddle spot. Jerky could swing right up and mount like nothing, but he was bigger and stronger than me. Jerky and I would likely move out west together someday. I'd have to catch up to his riding skills.

I rested my cheek on the horse's rough side and lifted my hands up onto his back. Quick, gotta do it quick. With all my might I hefted fast and hard, my belly teetering on his back. The animal took this just fine, my belly on his back, face flapping over the other side looking down at the earth. We settled like that, me resting there, more like the saddle than the rider.

A door slammed up at the house. Likely Pa having a night-restless smoke. I hoped he didn't check in my room, but that weren't likely. The slam made Lightning move and whinny a bit and I nearly slid off but somehow the movement jammed us together so I grabbed hold of his dark mane, swaying sideways then pulling around and snapping up like a doll, upright, clinging.

"We done that," I said, leaning down and whispering. "Let's get on before Pa sees."

I weren't as cold anymore, legs warm against the animal's sides. Then that house door slammed again, Pa cold and going into Ma's warmth. With the slam, Lightning started to walk, clomping out into the field, directionless into the blackness, toward the death and the secrets out there. We both turned our backs on the farm house, stepping solid across the bleak field. I held tight and felt the hunger of the animal come up into me. We stepped a little faster, pushing up into the vacant midnight jaw of some God's field, further, flesh on flesh, us two blistering into the night, and it felt like it did when I pressed into Jerky's back, hanging on when he galloped hard and hopped over a creek, my arms squeezing him and whooping like a bandit. I gave Lightning a little kick, thinking how I'd get Jerky on the back of my horse holding onto me for once, how we'd soar over a creek, how we'd ride all the way west. The kick shook Lightning and he gave his whole body a rough twist. I lost my grip and slid off flat on my side, smacking hard earth. Lightning stopped, turned and looked at me. And I swear that horse was grinning.

"All right," I said.

I turned back toward the barn, and Lightning followed.

4

Breakfast was a constant fuddle. Gran'd done it, stern and slick at the wood stove, hefting and ladling a pot of grits that would last through lunch. At dawn Ma was doing the chickens, feeding and gathering eggs, while Pa was doing nothing.

"Early mornings all women," Pa said. "Men ain't doing shit til they hit the field."

Fact was Pa'd didn't do no field work neither, not since Peepaw died. Peepaw'd done some good cropping, a few acres of corn in his day, but once he passed on Pa never took it up. I always thought farming was a noble thing, though not near as grand as the life of a cowboy. Since Ma was in the yard mornings, I got stuck with cooking breakfast.

"What shit slop you giving me Boy?" Pa said most every day since Gran's death.

The black iron pot sat on the flame and I cussed it softly, added more, added less, boiled it longer, threw in salt, even once spit in there thinking something had to give. I'd seen Gran cook it firm and fast every day, nothing to it, so why couldn't I get it right? Bad eating made Pa mad and I didn't like Pa mad. I tipped some out into Pa's bowl, then stepped back fast to avoid a flying fist. Sis got her ration. Ma came in, wiping her face, depositing eggs, sitting down and waving for coffee.

"Good," Pa said, shoveling the white gruel in his mouth fast like it was fixing to disappear.

"Told ya he'd get it right," was all Ma said, sipping her coffee and smiling over at Sis.

I sniffed at that damn pot. Nothing different today. No reason it should taste better. There was a window near the stove, opened a touch for steam, and I thought of the ride last night on the back of Lightning, that secret of ours. Horse was lucky. That's why the gruel tasted all right.

"No, horse is magic," Gran's voice said but I shooed it away.

Pa was rattling his bowl for more. "Get on to schooling," he said, taking his hand and shoving it into the bowl to test the temperature of the stuff.

Some days, if there was a lot of work tending the garden or tending to the animals, Pa told me to skip school. Ma'd up and promised the teacher Miss Sarah I'd go until I could read and write enough to get by outside of town, in case I wanted to leave. Ma was good that way, thinking of what might be good for her kids. Pa didn't mind as long as he didn't have to do nothing extra. Ma used her saved up egg money to get me a slate and piece of chalk for school.

Out the window, clouds skittered together and blocked the morning sun. Might snow. Was cold enough. I waited while they all sat and ate, huddled at the table that Pa made from a felled walnut tree. It was long and smooth and pretty. Could fit near ten people around it on Christmas.

Pa was a reed of a man, all bone really, with a shock of black hair and a really long jaw. His nose was long too, and his eyes were bright blue. Ma once said he looked like a king. He liked that. What kind of king I had no idea. Ma was pretty.

Her hair was thicker and darker than Pa's and she was taller than Pa and heavier too.

"Like me a big bear woman," drunk Pa had once said, grabbing hold of her tight and yanking her away.

Ma could lift a barrel filled with apples and she could walk miles in the snow if she needed to. She was strong like that.

"Got you a sturdy one, good thing," Gran used to say to Pa.

Sis was blonde and small for four years old and I loved her a mess. Even Pa was soft for her. Sweet little thing. I saw them three there, like a picture, and I was happy. I finished up the dishes once they got done, then dressed for school.

5

From the farm, the walk to school was a lick in spring, but mean and mule slow in the winter. Down the first hill of Black's Road was easy, but the second part of the journey was all uphill into hard wind. The wide patch of gray clouds had all but gobbled up the sun and the wind was making its way toward a storm. Near the top of the hill, Jerky slammed out from behind a tree. He yelled something, like he did every time he saw me coming up the hill. When she was pregnant, his Ma'd had a bad hankering for salty beef jerky, which is how he got his name. She swore it was all that ropey meat that made him so big and strong past his age of thirteen.

Jerky and I been best friends forever. He clomped down the hill toward me, head and shoulders thrust back, cheeks bright red and blond hair flying up like a mane while he blew steam on his hands to warm them.

"What you staring at knuckle head?" he said, coming up and punching me soft in the belly.

I was staring at his wide jaw, a man's jaw really, that big broad Peck nose and wide forehead thinking how he looked like a horse or some kind of Norseman warrior. I was itching to tell him all about Lightning. I wanted us to go riding together.

Pa liked Jerky's dad and brothers, which made things easy for us to be friends. If Pa hated somebody, the whole family had to hate them. Pa hated the Cleary clan and they hated us for the longest time, not sure why, but I knew if I stepped up on Cleary land at night I'd likely feel a bullet in my gut, no questions asked. The Pecks were all right though.

"Gonna be kissing for gold stars if you keep coming to school this much. Six days this month," Jerky said, looping his arm through my arm as we trudged up the hill to the school house.

Jerky had a way of doing things like that. Screaming with an ambush, then locking arms. Secretly, I figured Jerky was meant to be something important in life. He could read anything and he talked a blue streak. Brain smarts would help us when we traveled west. Pa always said you had to watch out for sneaky folks, men out there that were looking to knock the wind outta your dreams and steal the hat off your head.

Plus Jerky was strong and could already lick fellas older than him in a fight. He could throw a bale of hay like a feather, chop wood twice as fast as me, and swim Puddle Pond back and forth like a trout. In the summer, we'd skinny dip every chance we got, and this year I noticed the change in him, how much bigger he looked with all them muscles in his arms and legs.

"You want to see something?" he said.

I was waiting for the perfect moment to tell him about Lightning, to see the look on his face. He stopped at the top of the hill, turned away from the wind, and pulled something out from under his coat.

"I'll let you hold it but only for a bit," he said.

The wind set in with a new howling, and I was itching to tell him my surprise, but he thrust a book at me, giving me his crazy big-toothed smile.

"Tarzan, my Pa got it for me," Jerky said.

He was nuts for Tarzan, like I was nuts for Billy the Kid. I told him there were'nt no ape men out west, but he smacked me on the head and said we'd get to the jungle one day. He handed it to me slow and easy, like it might break. There was Tarzan, sitting up in a tree, one arm grabbing a branch, naked legs wrapped around a vine ready to swing. He was a fine-looking man, but still no Billy the Kid.

From Black's Road, we heard the school bell clang. Jerky grabbed back the book and set off. He hated being late. Me, I'd take my time, but the tearing wind gave me a kick in my step too, so I hurried after him. I'd have to tell him about Lightning later.

The school house was old, cold and ugly. It was one room with a tiny stove in the center. A long plank table for us kids. A chair and desk up front for Miss Sarah, who most folks said was right pretty, though she looked like every other buttoned-up lady to me. There was a chalk board and a big cross of Jesus. Gran said that way back the place had been a church, but that didn't last. One bitter winter they cut up the pews for fire wood. Nobody touched Jesus on his big cross though, out of fear.

"God don't want us freezing," Gran said.

Jerky and me joined the eight other kids at the long plank table watching Miss Sarah's back as she wrote numbers. Jerky poked me in the arm for no reason and Miss Sarah turned about. She was a tall woman, young but older looking with all that towering height. She wore long heavy dresses with big bright flowers splattered cross the front. Jerky said it was to keep our attention with the wind blowing around.

Miss Sarah asked a question and Jerky spit out the answer to that puzzle of numbers on the board before anybody even scratched. Miss Sarah nodded and set to piling up another batch of numbers, as if that first line weren't enough. The wind screeched high and loud, something awful, like a mighty hand smacking on the door. I thought of the devil and Gran and last night, secret riding in that black dead field, and I was scared. The wind kept up and there was a fierce battering at the window and Miss Sarah took a long pause.

"Well it's going to snow," she said, too softly really, as if she feared what it meant. "We might have a harsh one. Who wants to get up front and read?"

Jerky jumped up. While he recited aloud, that smashing fist of wind came again and kept going, long and steady, and Miss Sarah just shook her head then stopped Jerky. Storms came fast round here, and people got lost and they died.

"Get on home now," she said, her eyes soft and sort of sad looking.

Jerky and I were the first kids out the door, running with that beast wind slamming at us. I was trying to keep up with Jerky, wishing I could tell him about Lightning, but he was laughing at me and getting far ahead with them long legs of his. I kept chasing, but never caught him.

6

The sky tore open and threw buckets of ice down and the day got night and there was no more shadow, just hail and a wind that tore my face in half. I made it home at a fever pitch and went straight in. Ma was sitting alone at the table. She hopped up when she saw me and nearly knocked over her chair rushing to me, grabbing my hands. She had a mighty strong grip and a wild look in her eyes

"Youget on that horse and go get yer Pa fast as you can," she said.

There was a song in the house, the ice-stealing wind swashing across the place, going room to room. The walls rattled and Ma looked scared like the wind was some devil out to get us. She squeezed my hands even harder

"This one's come on fast Bud. You get! Go on!" she said. "He walked off to Puddle Pond to ice-fish, thinking to catch before the storm, damn fool."

I looked at her while that wind sang around us, and I knew she was looking at me like I was all of a sudden a man, not the boy from this morning. Peepaw froze to his death in a storm six years back, lost after a drinking night, fallen far off, gone.

I went out and stole across the field, the ice dancing with snow in my face and the clouds fat, low and fierce. My cheeks were hard and biting-red and my eyes stung with bits of ice. I busted into the barn, grabbing the saddle off the plow horse and the reins. Lightning looked dead at me. I had to get him bridled so I could lead us through the storm. His eyes were on mine and I stepped close and he knew, he knew what we had to do. I guided the muzzle over his head and he moved easy with me. Then I laid my cheek on his neck, struck fast with fear of facing that demon blizzard.

"This is your'n time," Gran's voice said.

I saddled up and guided us out. Ma was in the front of the house alone, looking like a tree losing leaves, swaying in that thin old dress. Her hair was flying, her arms folded. She didn't move, just watched us as we trotted against a white blindness that flung at us like wild, tangling fingers of death. I didn't turn to see her again, just got riding into the mess.

The daylight was lost now to that white darkness. It was like being in a locked cellar with one hot light pressing on my face. There was nothing more than the squealing wind in my ear and all the white and ice and meanness. It was bright but dark too. I couldn't see much up ahead. On the sides of things, past Lightning's flanks, I could make out the edges of the dirt road leading down from our house. We went slow. I knew the way to Puddle Pond by heart and could find it like a blind man knows where his Johnson's at, so that helped. Lightning was steady, moving at a good pace and I had my head bent low singing a little to him. We were trusting each other, and I knew our meeting last night was meant to ready us for this saving. The hill down from our house flattened out at Black's Road. We moved ahead.

The ride to Puddle Pond was all big ups and downs, gravel stretches and a lick across what Pa called Dead Field because the grass went short and black one blistering summer and never came back. I was blinded in the sleet but could feel the road under us. Lightning moved steadily, and I could tell we was hitting the first flat part of Black's Road because we got off the hill to our house and were on the first smooth patch.

For a second I thought I heard Ma, and something awful came up in me, my eyes stinging bad with the wind. I needed to turn in the saddle, to see Ma again, to see her shivering and waving at me to come back to the fire or see her standing there with Pa, all this suddenly a big mistake. My ass was near froze to the saddle and my whole body was stiff. I couldn't swivel back to see and a craziness came on me and I screamed to her. My open mouth took in the rush of snow and it got shoved down my throat with a fist that choked me and shut me up. Lightning led us forward and I thought *he knows better than me.*

The high-pitched singing noise in the wind came back as we went up Black's Road. I thought of Jerky just that morning, running out at me. I was inside of the storm alone, surely alone, since nobody with any sense would be out.

Rising up Black's Road toward the school house, we hit our first drift. Didn't seem possible snow could pile as tall as an army of men in such a short spell. It stretched clear across the whole of the road like a wall. I figured we was at the big curve, the spot where two oaks fell atop one another in a storm last spring, torn and yanked so they was forever tangled together like dead lovers. Looking sideways, I could barely see through the blowing snow. I heard that men stepped into these drifts, and those men went cold and found the drifts wider than they thought and they got confused and slept. Peepaw loved his whiskey and fell in this kind of storm. I wondered what it was he felt surrounded by ice and the bitter jaws of a last cold sleep.

Lightning paused, raised his head, and turned trying to see me. I leaned up and petted his head and he settled and moved into it. As we hit the drift, he made a screeching neigh and galloped through. It was a short one, and I thought he was one damn smart horse to know to push fast through like that.

We kept rising on the hill and my feet disappeared off my body. I tried to fetch them back by wiggling my toes in my boots. We passed the school house, I knew, since we sloped into a little dip in the hill that meant we would turn off soon toward Puddle Pond. There was no sun. My eyes stung something awful.

I steered Lightning right and we started clomping on gravel so I knew we was on the stretch before Dead Field. The gravel bounced us, which was good. It shook my body and my feet came back a little and the ride helped wake the gone parts of me. I clenched my wool covered fists over and over to keep them alive. The wind song went low and quiet and things felt deadly still. But in snow, the quiet was sometimes good. Like the hell of it had gotten whooped for a second and needed to rest its banging. In the quiet I could hear each step of Lightning and there was a soft bit of light, way above, making the gray sheet of clouds almost glow. For a scant second I though the sun might push out and warm things. But as we neared Dead Field, the wind picked up again and the screaming came high. More wetness and burning got at my cheeks and my feet disappeared again.

We turned into Dead Field, crunching on black grass, pressing ahead. Jerky and I had slid across patches of this field last winter. The grass was so short that it got slick like a frozed-up pond. Lightning's hoofs sunk onto it firm and we moved straight across. I knew Puddle Pond would come up soon and I got scared again.

Pa wouldn't just be sitting with his fishing pole waiting. He would of got up and started moving, heading back right away. The storm done came on like an avalanche. It threw so much so fast I didn't know what Pa would have thought. Lightning started to move faster, like he was hearing my thoughts, and I leaned into him and bounced higher in the saddle, moving straight toward the Pond. I started to yell high and loud, holding tight so I didn't fall off. "Get on, Get on!"

All at once the stinging wind and white was at my back and pushing me into it and I knew we were getting close to the spot. I felt a rising need to get at Pa, to grab him up. We got on faster and our bodies were racing in time and I felt us high up like sailing. Near the pond, I yanked Lightning and he reared back and neighed and for a second I thought I surely would fly off and land behind him, but we sank back down and settled.

We were both breathing hard and loud and again the wind settled and got softer in voice the way it felt in church, the breath of God. In the quiet, I saw something at the pond's edge: a person lying face down, hands stretched out toward something unseen. It could only be Pa.

7

He was lighter than I thought, small like me, and I was holding his body to mine like a twin. I knew when I first touched Pa he was gone, the froze death in his eyes, so I'd yanked him up into my arms and felt that hard cheek on mine. Something in me tore open then and the ice tears stung and we both fell over. I lay on top of him and didn't want to get up but knew that I had to keep moving, had to get back to Ma.

I stood up wobbling and looked down at him twisted in the snow. I kneeled and wanted to talk to him real bad but knew that I couldn't, and I spit and knelt and pulled him up and back into my arms, standing. He felt stiff and heavy like his insides were lead. For a second I thought of Gran, and I held him while the wind screamed. I wanted to scream along or maybe sing something like a hymn to rock him to sleep and send him to heaven.

I couldn't look at his face no more. The blowing snow made that near to impossible anyway. I used all my might to hoist him up and onto the back of my horse. I cajoled Lightning to stay still and not buck. I used the guide rope to fasten Pa's body down and hoped he didn't slide off. I was so froze I didn't think past the pain of tying the knots and knowing how long it would take to guide us home.

The blizzard was steady and mean, and it looked to be

a long one. One of them changing storms that gnaws down and makes its mark on things. I tried not to think of Ma or Sis as I struggled to guide Lightning back the way we came, his hoof prints covered in new snow. I held the lead firm and it was like Lightning was reaching through the rope, touching me, nudging me on.

"Keep on Boy," I heard Gran's voice say.

It was slow moving and I wanted to turn and keep an eye out that Pa didn't slip off, but I was afraid I might see his spirit bleeding out, reaching for the sky. I kept moving, steady and pained in the ice wind, and soon I couldn't hear nothing but my own breath and slow beating heart. There was nothing but white, endless white, and I listened for Gran but there was no more sound, like the air had gone too cold and thin even for her. There was nothing but Lightning and me. And that tied up body that used to be Pa.

8

There was a break in the blizzard, like it decided to take a breath and look down at what it had done, studying the frail piece of a man it tossed up to heaven's mouth. Laid out on the long kitchen table he built, Pa looked like a kid, all gentle and soft. He never had much weight on him, being bony and small like me. He started to melt. His body was cased in snow and a layer of ice, his face bone-white, lips blue, eyes froze shut. He looked real peaceful until the thawing started, making a pool of water all around him, trailing like a creek off the table sides. I was standing near him but had to step away so my feet didn't get wet. His iced-up hair lost its life, sinking in soaked strands. He somehow seemed deader now.

Gran used to say Pa's thick black hair weighed him and kept him from flying off in a storm. I wondered if he was with Gran, and if his voice might come at me like hers did after death. Not likely. Pa never spoke to me much in life. Didn't think he'd start jabbering in death. He was likely all cozy and warm, filling up with whatever kinda whiskey they served up there in the clouds, just taking it easy, which is what he liked best. Still, I couldn't quite conjure that he'd never cuss at me again.

The house was busy. Jerky and his Ma and Pa were there, and the Potter brothers had come, them two sitting outside in the cold talking low, drinking, smoking, bringing back all the best they could recall of Pa. Most folks knew them brothers as the tall Potter and the dumb Potter. Mr. Whittley and his wife Josephine and their two boys, who I never liked much, Jeb and Dill, they were there too. Whittley had a few glass jars of moonshine and set them under the table, just below Pa, as if he was gonna curl a dead arm right under there and get a last lick of it. I wouldn't put it past him.

Ma sat still. She'd put on a Sunday dress with these sweet little white flowers dancing all down the front of it, and I thought they looked like snowflakes but I didn't say nothing. Jerky's Ma sat right next to her, holding her hand and ever so often leaning over and whispering. Baby Sis was on the floor like a cat at Ma's feet. I stayed away, hanging by the door with Jerky, keeping my distance from both Ma and Pa. The Whittleys, who had a little bit more of everything than most folks because of the fineness of their moonshine, had brought deer meat and Josephine was cooking.

The storm was keeping still and I felt Jerky's hand patting my shoulder and I pushed it away to let him know he didn't need to do nothing. He was nervous that way, anytime something went wrong he'd start-in doing stuff, like he thought he could fix it by pressing on it until the bad thing flew out like a splinter in your foot. I was glad he was there though. I heard the Potter brothers on the porch gabbing about the storm. The dumb one said how maybe Pa's death had stopped it.

"No way this uns' just got its teethen us, it's gonna stick a spell," said the tall Potter.

Then Ma stood up.

"I ain't gonna burn him."

Her words were slow and loud, and her body tight and

high and big like it was filling with air. Then the whole of her shuddered and withered inward like a fast dying flower and she snapped her head down and the wailing of grief came on her and Jerky's Ma swooped in like she'd been waiting for it. The two fell into each other like a dancing couple and the swaying started and the place was filled with the most awful sound. Just then, the storm threw down new hail that brought the Potter brothers in. I was glad for the hail's noise. I let Jerky pat me awhile, and just stood there in a long breath of something I could barely stand, a welling up inside that felt like it could kill me. I couldn't look over at Pa no more, I couldn't look nowhere, and I wished Gran's voice would come but the only sound was Ma's terrible wailing and the beating hands of the storm.

9

I didn't know nothing about a proper burying in the earth. Still it had to be done. I fetched an old shovel and a pitchfork from the barn cause that's all we had. I didn't want to get to digging right off so I stood still and got a look at my horse in his stall. His face was still and his eyes clear and sad like he knew. I wanted to press my face to him and just rest there, but I had the death work. I went out to the field where we were gonna do it. Jerky and the Potter brothers were waiting on me. It was dusk by then. The Potter brothers weren't much for hefting anything other than a moonshine jar, but they were fond of telling anybody who'd listen how to do things.

"Gotta get in there hard Boy, shove it like ya screwing," the tall Potter said, jar sipping and hugging himself in the cold while Jerky and I started to dig. "Earth that mean ain't gonna open up to ya without a fight, just like a woman."

"Them two ain't seen no screwing," said the dumb Potter, snorting.

"You shut it. He lost his Pa," tall Potter said softly.

We were out in the field behind the house. We'd cleared a good square of snow and had set to stabbing icy earth. The shovel barely made a dent but I kept on. In the distance I could see Ma in my bedroom window watching with Jerky's Ma, their small heads together. I'd always been afraid of this field, like it held the dead. Now it would.

"Damn it Boy, give it to me," tall Potter said.

I reached out with the shovel but kept my fist on it as he grabbed it.

"You call me Bud. Pa's gone, I ain't no Boy," I said, and far off I heard Gran's voice humming.

He nodded and took the shovel and went at the earth with fast strokes. He was stabbing and huffing, cussing a bit, then blowing out air and making sounds like an animal or a distant runaway train. Then he started yelling.

"Get you, you, you get on," tall Potter said looking at the ground.

He was screaming, louder and louder, his arms heaving faster attacking the hard earth.

"Come on you, get on that now," he yelled to Jerky.

Jerky looked on, then started to peck hard with his pitchfork. Soon he was yelling loud as tall Potter.

"Get get get it, come on get on her, deee haaaa!" tall Potter said and Jerky said it too, repeating.

They were swaying like crazy scarecrows come alive, yowling all sorts of stuff, and the earth looked like it just had to give soon. Finally it started to crack a little and then dumb Potter started screaming too and jumping up and down and then I heard myself, my voice going deep and ragged and joining in.

"Get it, get get get, deeee haaaaa!" I said and was on tall Potter, my hands over his, our bodies side by side, both a hold of that shovel and punching at the mean black crow dirt.

I forgot the cold and my mind flew on while I screamed, while we all screamed, and I forgot about Ma at the window. I felt dizzy and my head was buzzing, like some set of insane flies had crept in there and were dancing, and in this death rush I knew I could forgive anything I'd been holding deep at Pa. I felt Gran at my arm too, pressing. We ranted like derelict preachers, all four of us, caught in a cold crazy jig, and the earth finally heaved inward and gave all the way, letting rise its softer, female under-blackness that would let us keep pushing until we went deep enough to bury my Pa. As the earth shifted I heaved out a rail of dumb tears and I wailed my grief loud enough for heaven to hear.

10

In the days that followed, Ma took to her room, Baby Sis at her side most of the time. The sky got ice blue but nothing melted. Trees were heaped with snow and everything was dipped in ice. Red and blue birds swooped down in the morning and pecked at the white, then blew up high again, beaks empty.

Jerky showed up one fine clear morning wearing a coon skin coat, a jack rabbit hat and dungarees fixing to split at the seams. Jerky always looked like he was shoe horned into his duds, on account of how he grew like a rag weed. His Pa said he'd need to bust out of his pants and boots before he got a new pair.

I was mighty glad to see him. I'd been stir-crazy in the house and felt mad at something I couldn't figure out. He looked at me for a minute, then pulled me rough and close to him, hugging me long, too long like he wanted to squeeze the loss out of me. He was tall so my cheek squashed up on his chest and I could hear his heart beating. I could smell him too, and feel his big hands across my back, and I didn't really want to move, thinking if we could stay like that then the bad death day would be gone. I shut my eyes and saw Jerky and me side by side out west, our horses tethered together, then he said a real soft "sorry" and something skittish stirred in me, something I'd felt a few times since summer when he and I was alone, so I yanked away and laughed like a dumb kid. He dropped his head, in some silent nod to Pa, and I shuddered with a rush of knowing how lucky I was to have a friend like Jerky. He was waiting for me to make a move, and I remembered I hadn't properly introduced him to Lightning. He'd only got a glimpse of him the day we hauled in Pa after the storm.

"Come on," I said.

We tromped through the snow and I thought of my last icy trek, Lightning and me blinded, moving in that bad storm toward Pa. But the sun was bright now, and things felt clear like I was turning toward something new, like some spring was possible. Being long-legged, Jerky moved faster than me, but I kept a pace so I could lead us into the barn. I shoved the door open and the light got soft, that soothing smell of hay and horse slowing everything down.

"Let's get a good look at your new horse, Bud!" Jerky said.

He pushed ahead of me and went right over and put his hands to Lighting, running his palm across my animal, stroking his thick tail, touching his ear. Jerky looked like he could hop right up with ease, which irked me something fierce. I pushed him aside.

"This is my horse, Lightning," I said.

I was starting to tell him how we rode to find Pa when Jerky put both his big hands on Lightning's back and hoisted himself up and over, striding. As he did there was an awful rip and Lightning jerked his head and Jerky let out a yelp and I started laughing. He done tore his pants.

"I didn't say you could get on him, serves ya right," I said.

"Hell, I got on my long johns. You want me to teach ya to ride," Jerky said. "Once we get out west we gonna have to be ready to fly. You don't know nothing about riding, Bud."

He looked mighty fine up top there, towering over me, his high rabbit hat and fancy coat, even with the tear from crotch to knee, showing off his big thighs and thermals, he looked like a bonafide cowboy. I had some catching up to do.

"Get yer saddle," Jerky said, giving Lightning a few nick coos to guide him out of the barn.

Going for my saddle, I passed our old plow mule Bess and wondered what we'd do come spring, how we'd keep up the garden without Gran or Pa. I wondered if Ma ever thought of cropping the fields for corn again like Peepaw used to. My dream of going west was always partly to get away from Pa. Now there was only Ma and Baby Sis and it seemed more like running from them, which was a lot different than running from Pa.

The barn door shucked open and Lightning pressed his nose out. That bold late winter sun cast a wild glow around Jerky, giving him a strange brightness and something akin to beauty. I followed the two out, paying no attending to the low, sad cry of a far-off coyote.

Jerky got me to canter then gallop cross the field on Lightning before I fell on my ass. He laughed a lot, which irked me, but he was a good teacher. After my second fall, we took a break at the crest of Pritch Hill where an old monster oak tree lived. It was a grand spot looking down on the wild peach orchard that was all branch bones and iced trunks. We'd feast on them peaches in summer. The riding warmed us a bit, so we could afford to sit a spell in the cold sun. We both fit side by side against the oak's mighty trunk. Jerky pulled a rolled cigarette and a match and lit it like he was in a saloon, then he passed it to me.

"A few things we need to know fore we go west, Bud."

I looked at the skinny smoke with the red tip.

"Go on," he said.

I sucked in a burnt breath that scorched my throat and passed it back.

"Do all cowboys gotta smoke?" I said, coughing.

Jerky drew long, looked out at that lean stretch of peach trees below, then let out a cloud.

"I think so," he said.

He pulled out a flask from his coon coat. I'd tasted shine, but only a nip. I knew how it made Pa crazy so I never drew more than a bit.

"For your Pa," Jerky said, titling and slugging.

He handed it off and I took a drink, the moonshine fire burning over and past the raw feeling still stuck in my throat from the smoke.

"For Pa," I said.

Lighting was behind us, watching, almost like a preacher keeping his flock. I wondered if we could take Lightning with us out west. Jerky was having another pull of the shine.

"How we fixing to get there?" I said.

The wind drew a new breath, peach trees leaning.

"Well," Jerky said.

He passed me back the flask, then stretched his arm out across my shoulder. He let it rest there and I fought my urge to lean into him, to shut my eyes and hear his heart. I sucked on the flask and felt that warmth.

"We could hop the railroad," Jerky said. "But now you

got a horse, we could ride."

I thought of us riding side by side. Jerky gave my shoulder a squeeze and the wind rose high pitching that big oak's branches and I let my head fall to the side, on Jerky's chest. My head felt scorched and empty from the shine. Jerky started to sing real soft.

"At the booly wooly wild west show," he sang.

He moved his hand up to my forehead, then brushed my hair, petting it back. I kept my eyes shut, falling into that touch, letting my head drop a little further, like I was sinking right under his skin, he and I one cowboy now, riding fast and hard past any steaming train, fast and free into some endless God plain.

11

Ma was sitting in the main room. The fire had died out so the place was freezing. I got at that greasy black stove and stoked up the heat. She had on the same dress she wore at the funeral with them funny snowflake flowers. Her hands were folded and she was staring at the kitchen table that Pa had made and that he'd been lying on dead not so long back. There was a letter lying in front of her on the table.

"Gert's coming," she said. "I got the letter in the post."

I knew nothing about Ma's fancy sister, other than that she'd sent Ma and Pa money to build our house and sometimes folks hushed when they started talking about her. I figured she was a bad woman, the way heads and eyes dropped when her name tumbled out. Plus Gran always crossed herself.

"Gert's a hard un," Ma said, hands still folded, eyes down. "She ain't like us but she's rich. Real rich. She gonna help us."

She looked up at me.

"And we need help, Bud."

I sat at the table, small like a boy in size but feeling grown now, sitting next to her trying so hard to look ready to take charge of whatever came my way. I tried to think what Pa would do. Get drunk likely. I wanted to hear Gran something awful, but there was only the hard wind.

I took a breath and reached over and put my hands on her shoulders, pulling her to me. She resisted at first, shaking, then she gave in and set to crying. I let her wail, cause I knew she needed to. I'd never been too fond of Pa, him always getting at me for something, but I knew he was everything to Ma. She shook in my arms, and I felt a bigness in me and knew it was all gonna change now. Holding Ma, her all wrecked up and shivering, I tried to think of what it was we might do to get along. I saw my dreamed-on plan to go west dim down and I felt ashamed. I thought of them long-ago crops planted by Peepaw and our land.

The past few years, I'd helped Ma with the chickens and Gran with the gardening. Pa'd always got us by, selling the eggs, and getting jobs on nearby farms. Once he went off for three months on a digging gig.

Ma shook and rocked in my arms like a kid. She was bigger than me, but shivering with all that sadness made her bones thin. I tried to guess what Gert would look like but I came up with nothing. I heard myself saying Shhh over and over.

"When?" I said.

Ma pulled her head up, then looked around like she was just noticing me there. She sat up tall again, and put her hands together.

"She's on her way on a ship. Docking in New Orleans, then she's gonna drive here," Ma said. "She got an automobile."

A thrill shot up my back. The Whittleys had a tractor but I never got on it. I never seen an automobile. Jerky said he was buying a Model-T someday but I never thought I'd see one anytime soon.

"Didn't know a lady could drive," I said.

"She got a friend," Ma said. "They gonna buy a horse here too."

Ma got up and she let her head fall back and her long thick black hair spill all around her. I thought she looked like a statue. I'd never really sat alone with Ma. There'd always been folks or Baby Sis and always something to do. Standing there, I thought she looked right young.

"Gonna be all right, Bud," she said. "They gonna take my room. You come out here where Gran used to sleep. I'll get in there with Sis. Gert's always been good to me. Better than I been to her."

She turned and went back into her room, moving slow but steady, that long girlish hair sweeping across her back, that sad dress of dying flowers fading out in the evening light.

12

The day Gert arrived Ma was flitting around crazy. Baby Sis
was at her heel, them both riled, flapping their arms like wild
birds. It was like something had caught fire between them
two and they was fanning to put it out. We'd been cleaning
all week. Floors, stove, windows, the whole mess. I weren't
too pleased to give over my bed and take up Gran's old
board and blanket but it was not far off from the stove, which
Gran said she liked. I couldn't help but feel some excitement
nipping at me. When evening came I wondered if something
had gone wrong, or if Gert got stuck out there on the ocean.
Or maybe she wasn't coming at all. I went to the barn to be
alone.

Lightning was standing alert in his stall like he was
waiting for me. I grabbed a curry comb to get at a mess
of burrs, then finished up with a soft bristle brush on his
back and sides. Since I been riding him, practicing what
Jerky taught me and tending him, his coat was shinier and
he looked stronger. I stroked his back and could feel him
shudder a little. Jerky had been busy with his Pa all week
cropping, and I was missing our rides together. I hoped he'd
come by soon.

"This lady might just be crazy," I said to Lightning.

I leaned my face on his side and put my hand by his
heart. He heaved a hot breath and I felt like I could see inside

his head, the way I got under Jerky's skin that day by the old oak. All the sudden Lightning's head popped straight up and his body stiffened. Things were still for a moment, then I heard it. A rattling, barking noise coming from the distance. It sounded like something metal being chopped and sawed, or like the airplane we saw at the Lowell County fair once. Lightning was shivering a little and I patted him, waiting. The rattling came louder and harder and I held onto my horse. There was a loud screech, then it stopped and I heard voices. They were muffled through the barn door, but somebody was shouting. I headed out and watched from a distance.

The automobile looked like some slick black bullet, but the lady who had to be Gert standing by it was all bursts of color. The car's yellow lamplights were on and shot into the field like bolts of fire. A tall, fancy looking man was hauling a trunk out of the back of the car. Gert was gussied in a get-up like I'd never seen, wearing a long coat with fur on the collar and a big hat and heeled shoes and something that sparkled. Ma flew toward her. Gert seemed to hesitate, then she moved into the car's lamplights. She was bigger than Ma, tall and fit like a lady athlete, but with that crazy hat that had a huge feather in it. I could see that her hair was the color of sorghum syrup. I caught her looking at me and her face was all sharp angles. She looked sort of funny, not real like Ma or Miss Sarah, more like a lady in a Sears catalogue. Gert held Ma and the two rocked in and out of that car's hard yellow light, caught in the glow of it, and I thought Ma was crying.

Gert's friend was there by the car's light too, standing alone, and he was almost as fancy as her. He had black wavy hair and a real big mouth sucking a cigarette. He was tall and everything about him was grand, but at the same time there was something strange, soft and too pretty for a fella. Like a dandy man in the film reels. Maybe it was the way he stood there like he was posing. He sure didn't look nothing like any man I'd ever seen and I had an urge to go and see him up close but I waited. He nodded my way and sucked the cigarette in his wide lips. I felt more scrawny than ever. Ma had said a fella was coming with Gert, but I figured it'd be some hired hand or driver. He weren't no hired hand.

He came toward me, leaving the women there. He was wearing a dirt colored, thick looking suit with bright gold buttons and a vest and even a felt hat. His shoes had long ugly points and the muscles in his arms pressed at the suit coat as he moved like the whole thing might bust off of him. He tossed his cigarette to the ground.

"I'm Mr. Nadir," he said.

He reached out his big hand for me to shake. He wore gloves the color of milk. I stood like a fool, shifting. I saw Baby Sis giggling and waving just inside the house. I moved over to him and reached out my hand. When he took it, I felt a strong squeeze, and in his eyes something curious.

"Good to meet you," he said.

Ma and Gert made their way toward the house, arms locked.

"Bud come in and get the fire going and let's get some food hot," Ma said.

I went out back to get some more wood for the stove while Mr. Nadir hauled Gert's trunk into the house.

13

Dawn came like a kick in the head after a night with my back on the cold floor, stove dead and wind spitting through the walls. I thought the voice that got me up was Gran's, but it weren't.

"We're going to see a horse," said Gert.

She was buttoned up all business and serious, with the sun itself barely awake. I rubbed my eyes, got a good look at her, and bust a gut. She was dressed like a man.

"Haven't you seen a woman in pants?" Gert said.

"Heck no," I said.

She was wrapped up in thick wooly stuff. The pants had fat cuffs and the jacket matched, plus there was a white shirt, a long coat and another crazy hat sitting up high like a man's derby. She had a long scarf wrapped around her neck.

"I told him we'd be early. We'll eat in town," Gert said, then went out the door.

I pulled on pants and my flannel shirt, wondering where the heck that woman thought we'd eat, with half a mind to wake Ma. The house was still. I put some branches and a big log in the stove and stoked it, so they'd have heat for waking. They'd set a spot for Mr. Nadir on a pile of blankets on the floor near me and he was rolled up tight, stiff and dead asleep. I figured he weren't going with us. Late last night, when everybody was asleep, Gert had snuck out and knelt by him on the floor. I'd stayed still and seen her lean close and whisper things in his ear, then stroke his cheek a few times before she went back to her room. I never known a woman to do like that to no man that weren't her husband. Maybe that's why we never heard much about Gert. I guess she weren't no Christian lady. After that, I laid awake a long time, thinking Mr. Nadir might get up and come talk to me, to ask me something, kneeling close and whispering low. But he didn't.

A horn blew. I laced up my boots. In daylight, the contraption they drove looked like a box with two big wheels in front and two scrawny ones in back. She'd got it going and was sitting in the driver's seat. She expected me to get in, I figured. It had a top to it and glass in the front but the sides of the jalopy were wide open. One bump and I'd fly out. The long back seat inside was fancy looking and I wondered how they kept it all so spit shined. Gert had on a pair of goggles and looked like some crazy bug. The machine was rattling and coughing, I was sure it was gonna blow up. I turned around to see Ma in the doorway.

"Go on, she needs your help," Ma said, holding her robe closed. "It's all right."

I moved toward that mad woman and her snickering machine, took a breath, crossed myself, and stepped in. She had it going right away and we were tripping down the gravel toward Black's Road. I was sure we'd topple at any second.

She shouted at me like we was old pals, "Haven't been in anything like this I take it?"

"Didn't figure women could drive," I said, my hand clenched tight on the seat front, knuckles red.

"We will likely get the vote too you know," Gert said.

When we shifted onto the snow-covered dirt of Black's Road the thing wavered side to side, like a sick mule, and I wanted to tell her to stop, but she started laughing real loud and we kept on. We were moving fast, swaying, and I thought I might be sick myself, but once we climbed the hill and passed the school house, I settled. The cold air got under my coat and I tried to stay still and not shiver. I wondered what Jerky would think if he saw us rattling by.

"Your mother said you're good with horses, that true?" she said.

I considered the idea, mostly because Ma said it and I never thought she had me much in her head. I kept the thing growing between Lightning and me almost secret.

"Don't know," I said. "I got a horse."

We curved on the road, past a wide smack of iced up woods, all white and frozen like somebody went in and painted every branch with fancy wedding cake icing. The car had settled its burping and was moving smoother. I noticed her gloves on the steering wheel. There were white like the snow, soft like a pale buttery hide, and they had the letter G sewn into the top with red thread.

"We'll eat first. There's a restaurant in town, right?"

There was Ethel's. I'd never been. It was near the store and a bar Pa went to when he won big at poker. Gert turned and gave me a long stare, which made me nervous since I don't like to be looked at plus she wasn't watching the icy road.

"You don't say much do you?"

"You know horses," Gran's voice said, coming up on me unexpected, like a dreamy whisperer at midnight.

"I know horses," I said.

Gert nodded and got back to watching the road. I stared straight ahead and wondered what I might eat at Ethel's.

14

They all stared at us when we walked in, the two young cowboys eating, old Lady Wilcox who lives in town, and even Ethel at the counter. Couldn't blame them. Gert was a sight, all tall and warrior-like wearing men's pants and pulling up in that noisy jalopy. And me, twerpy and shuffling next to her. Gert swung up to the counter and got right into talking to Ethel, who was pouring coffee. I lagged and finally sat, getting another look at the cowboys. Ethel was already laughing loud at something Gert had said. Her face was fat and wrinkled, spotted with red cheek paint, and her pink and white waitress outfit was tight and busting across the front. Ethel was a widow whose husband left the place to her. Folks said she was a little crazy but made good pie.

"Eggs and grits all right?" Ethel said, like they were sisters sharing a secret.

Gert nodded and I sat quiet, not sure what I was supposed to do.

"He's timid," Gert said. "Bring him eggs and bacon."

Ethel laughed out loud again and left us. I wished I'd stayed at home, though I couldn't recall the last time I'd ate bacon and that part sounded right good.

"How old are you?" Gert said as Ethel put down two coffee mugs.

"I'll be thirteen," I said, wanting to sound as old as I

could.

Gert sipped the muddy coffee and studied me again like she'd done in the car. I stole a look at the cowboys. One was rolling a cigarette. I'd have Jerky teach me how to do that.

"You're jockey size, small like your Pa," she said.

"What's that supposed to mean?"

"Just an observation," Gert said. "I breed race horses, Bud. You're good riding size."

Her face was gentle so I calmed down, and for a second I even thought of Gran, but then Ethel slammed down china plates full of food and Gert turned away. I ate slow at first, starting with the bacon, feeling plenty guilty that I couldn't give some to Ma and Baby Sis. It tasted so good though that I fast forgot them both and shoveled it in before somebody grabbed it back. Gert ate fast too, saying stuff between bites. The food settled me and by the time we left, I was half excited to see the horse she meant to buy. I wanted to ask Jerky what the hell a jockey did.

The two cowboys got up. They were both lanky, wearing dusty chaps and plaid shirts One of them stretched his arms way over his head moaning a little, his shirt hitched up showing a long skinny scar across his flat belly. He caught me looking at him.

"Come on," Gert said.

15

I'd heard tell of the Hughes family, dark whispery stories about things done that couldn't be undone, bad women that had to be sent off, and men with so much money they had bathtubs lined with gold. Folks said they made their first fortune in oil, then raised cows for slaughter. The horses were just for show and racing.

Their farm was a ways off from town, past the empty flat lands. In truth, there weren't no real Hughes for miles, just men that ran their place, bred their fancy horses, corralled their cows, and shoveled their money in buckets. I'd heard from Jerky that most of the family lived in New York. Maybe Gert knew them.

We left Gert's car at the farm entrance since the road was all chucked up. We walked the last bit, past a three-story house, out to where the stables sat. It was a clear, cold morning, the sky that bright blue that made it seem like it oughta be warmer. A pack of swallows were swishing around high up in a big oak that had lost some of its ice. The ground was dusted white, but they done cleared away the big drifts and piles of snow. Gert led us toward a tall reedy guy wearing a big cowboy hat and a skinny little jacket. He was smoking, smiling like the wind didn't slice at him.

"Don't say anything," Gert said in a low, dark voice.

I nodded, thinking what the hell am I gonna say to some

crazy man fixing to freeze. Pa always said men who wore cowboy hats ought to go to Texas. We're farmers, he'd say, though I never seen him do much farming. I never had the guts to tell him what I was thinking: I'm going west old man, I'm buying me a cowboy hat.

The skinny guy was leaning on a fence circling the corral. We got to the fence and followed his eyes. The horse was standing still. It was deep, rich and as black as prime plowing earth, shiny in the sun, with a soft mane of hair that swept over onto its back. Its nostrils were like big perfect triangles of tar, shooting out cold air. There was one diamond shaped patch of white, like spilled cream, on its forehead. I'd never seen anything so beautiful.

"That's him?" Gert said, leaning into the fence, standing close to the cowboy.

"Yes Ma'am," he said. "Straight Egyptian black colt. Smooth topline and hip, excellent tail-carriage and motion. Well broke."

The animal stayed still there, like a library book painting, and I shifted in the cold.

"Ready to ride?" Gert said.

I looked at that animal, then at Gert.

"It's yours," Gran's voice said.

"I got a rider, you ain't thinking that kid's gonna get on that prime animal," the skinny guy said, touching the brim of his hat like that made what he said more important.

"He'll ride," Gert said.

"No," the cowboy said.

Gert took a deep breath, then turned to go.

"What you doing?" he said.

Gert turned. I hadn't moved. She walked slowly toward

the fella, then got right up close to him.

"If you're looking to sell, my boy will ride him. If you're wasting my time tell me now," she said.

He looked like he was gonna touch the brim of his hat again, but instead he huffed, spit and lit another cigarette.

"I'll get the saddle," he said.

Gert and I stood at the fence. The horse didn't move. I felt scared and sick like all that sweet bacon was gonna fly right back out of me, like hail bursting from the sky.

"I ain't rode nothing that perfect," I said softly.

Gert went over to the gate and let herself in, then motioned me over. We walked toward the horse and still it didn't move, which I thought was awful strange. It got more and more like a picture book horse the closer we got, pecks of snowflake white on its hooves, a peaking back arch and every bit of his body hard and lean. Gert stopped near the animal, then motioned me on.

"Get a good look," she said.

I stepped up and the wind stood still and the horse turned to me. The ice under my boots felt soft and I could feel my own breath. It was a mighty thing. I touched him like the first time I held Baby Sis, feeling that soft thrill of being near something so perfect. I could barely stand it. The shivers swarmed over me and I thought I might fall, but the warm feel of him took me closer and I felt the hot air blowing at me from his nostrils and I was quiet.

The cowboy was coming with the saddle.

"Give it to him," Gert said.

"There's a scar on his eyelid," I said.

I could see a tiny jagged scar. Gert turned to the cowboy while he handed me the saddle.

"Birth scar, ain't nobody put hands on that horse. Perfect health," he said. "All the best got marks."

I saddled him up and looked into the blackness of his hide, scared to get up but at the same time aching to, wanting to ride this mighty horse.

"Take her out and get a good gallop in," Gert said.

The cowboy sighed, lit another cigarette, then put out his cupped hands and hoisted me up. Gert laughed and took him by the arm like they was long lost lovers. She led him back out of the corral, leaving me sitting on that black beauty like I owned him. It was like being on top of a mountain, not at all like saddling up on my Lightning. My legs laid on him and I could feel every breath. He was waiting for me to do something, so I nudged him and we went right into a trot. My body sat up high and everything Jerky taught me was there, his hands touching mine showing me rein work, his voice urging me to take a chance.

We trotted away from the coral, toward empty white plain, and I nicked him, stiff on the reins, thrusting my shoulders back, feeling that ride. I'd never imagined an animal could move to speed so quick yet feel so gentle. I leaned deep in, holding steady, getting my face down and ripping into the push with this beauty. We were far away from the corral and out into a clear sweet grassy plain, nothing but white ground and a sky cracking open with blue. He was moving like no animal could, like his body was one rhythm flying fast and the wind was part of him. I just stayed with him and the field bled so far and fast, the trees off both sides blurs of green. Toward a hill, I felt a new thrill rise through me from my feet straight up to my head, a shivering and crazy freedom. At the hill we slowed, I reared gently and we turned together and I felt his heat, the strength of us together. We took it at a slow trot, back toward Gert and the cowboy, in no hurry at all.

We got to the corral and Gert was waiting. She came up and ran her hand along the horse's flank.

"Well?" Gert said.

"You best buy him," was all I could manage.

I rested my hand on the horse's neck.

"You need to come down," Gert said.

I looked at her like we'd just met.

The skinny cowboy came over and stood close, grinning. He was younger than I first thought. The weather had burnt and creased his face, but he had a strong jaw and big bright eyes and wasn't so far past twenty.

"Yeah, he got ya," the cowboy said.

I couldn't meet his eyes anymore so I got down and he led the horse out of the corral. Gert caught up with him and they headed off to put the horse back in its stable then get on to the main house to finish the deal.

I turned back once toward the stable but there was nothing to look at. I wanted to run back and touch that horse again, mount it and ride off to find Jerky, get him high up there with me, behind me, showing him how a perfect animal feels when there's nothing but wind and horse and us. I stood there feeling lost until I heard Gert holler for me to get on.

16

Back home I was itchy all day, wanting to get off and talk to Jerky, but I was behind on my chores since we'd been out all morning. Gert bought the horse but left it at the Hughes for the time being. I couldn't bring myself to go see Lightning. It was like I'd cheated on him, gone and run my mouth along the backside of a secret lover. I finally got my chores done and ate, then I headed off to bed feeling bushed. Lying still, that black Egyptian horse of Gert's swarmed over me, and half sleeping, I felt his hooves on my chest and needles of horse hair in my eyes and I woke and looked out my window at the night stars. They swept across the blackness like a tail reaching to some dark angel.

"You awake?" Ma said.

I sat up and shook that dream horse off me. In the corner, the moon throwing light, Ma looked pale as snow, but her face was in a dark shadow. I couldn't see her eyes, which gave me a scare, like they'd been plucked out. I sat up, got my socks on, and pulled my pants up over my nightshirt.

"Come on," Ma said.

I followed her into the hall, her shoulders hunched low and sad like they were the day Pa died. We went into the main room where Gert and Mr. Nadir sat drinking at the kitchen table. The stove fire was stoked and flaming. Mr. Nadir had added wood. It seemed he was good for something other than sitting around in dandy clothes and smelling good. Ma sat and I stood looking at the three of them. Mr. Nadir got up, all broad shoulders and slick hair and jawbones. He lit a cigarette.

"Family matters, I'll leave it to you Gert," he said, going to the door.

"Sit," Ma said to me.

She and Gert were side by side at the big table Pa built, and I sat across from them on a long eating bench. You could see the sister in them. They both had the long tall frame and that thick dark hair. Gert was smiling, her eyes lit with the fire. Ma looked like she might up and ball any minute. I didn't like it.

"I've got a proposition for you," Gert said.

She held a glass of liquor in her hand. Ma's hands were folded and she lowered then slowly lifted her head, pulling up a hidden strength she had been keeping out of sight. Her face filled with color and heat and she brought her eyes to mine.

"Listen good, Bud," Ma said.

Gert drank, then spoke slowly. "I've got to get my new show horse back to New York and I want you to go with me. Horse needs a rider and I can see it in you. Once we're there we can see what else there is in you."

Ma kept her eyes on me and her face colored. Then she reached across the table and took my hand in hers and held it tight. I heard Gran too. "Your time boy," she said.

"This is a real chance, Bud," Ma said. "You hear me?"

"You'd get room and board and good pay. Enough to send money home," Gert said. "I can see how you love horses. I think you might be a substantial young man someday and

I'm willing to take a chance on you."

Ma had a good grip on my hand and I wanted to get up and hug her, get closer to her, feeling all the sudden a rush of ghosts everywhere, Pa, Gran, even Peepaw like something new was being born and dying all at the same time. I lowered my head and Ma gave my hand a squeeze and I thought of Jerky, his hand cross my shoulder up there on Pritch Hill, talking about going west.

"I'm giving your mother money to keep things going here, so you don't need to worry about her," Gert said. "But you got to decide right off. We're heading out tomorrow with my Egyptian. Time's wasting. That's how it is."

Gert turned and went to the door, calling out for Mr. Nadir. She stepped out and left Ma and me alone and I was shivering, not feeling that flaming stove, just the touch of Ma's hand in mine.

"Sis and I will be all right here," Ma said real loud and firm. "I got the Potter brothers near and can bring on Jerky to do chores for pay. Sometimes life throws you a chance, Bud. You don't always get another one."

She squeezed my hand harder and leaned close. I wanted to say something good but I was stung hard by this whole thing and by her saying Jerky's name, conjuring that losing.

I shut my eyes and all I could feel was the flat inside of Ma's hand and her soft voice telling me it was good, it was good, and all I could see was that frothing black horse, hooves on me, yanking me and racing away from the place I called home to a glittering place I knew nothing about.

17

I fought sleep hard. I wanted to stay up all night, finding my way through this bright new mess. But night kept at me and dreams fired up, like Gran burning. I'd dream and wake, try to sit up, then slump back into it. I was on that Egyptian horse, riding faster than I ever rode before, and I was a different version of me, older and stronger and screaming something but every time I woke up I couldn't remember the words. I could smell that animal on me. Finally I got up, dressed and snuck out to the barn. I had to stay on my feet, to figure this out. Lightning was waiting for me.

"What am I gonna do, boy?" I said.

He leaned forward in the stall, and I swear he was gonna tell me something like Gran, get those big eyes in my head and say *this is what you do, Bud*. But he just sniffed at me, and I pressed my cheek on his face.

I saddled him and we rode out into the night. It wasn't far to Jerky's house. I started slow, but moved faster, like I was back in that dream, a cowboy chasing something. The Pecks had a big spread at the bottom of Whiskey Road. I always wondered if Pa was the one who named that. The house was dark. I tethered Lightning and went round the back to Jerky's window on the second floor. He and I had snuck out a few times last summer, night swimming. I hunted around for a pebble, then heard him call.

"Bud?"

He was leaning out his window, watching me. I could see him bright in the moonlight and my heart raced and I knew he'd know what to do once I got to him. I waved and he scurried down the roof, landing on his feet.

"What you doing out?" he said. "I couldn't sleep."

We was standing close, staying quiet and all the sudden everything went fire white, like somebody gut punched me, and I thought don't you dare Bud but the tears came on and then I was sobbing and Jerky was yanking me fast to the barn out back. His Pa was mean if you woke him.

In the barn, Jerky latched the door lock and we sat in a pile of hay near the horse stall and I tried to stop crying, but there was something bigger than me, something too fierce and strong and I couldn't breathe right, couldn't even see right, but I felt Jerky's arm across my shoulder and I just fell hard a hundred miles down.

"Come on," he said, soft and close like he could heal this wreck in me.

But it only got worse, me wailing and shaking and Jerky's horse neighing at us and Jerky let me lean into him more. Then I sat up and he was looking at me and nothing made sense.

"I can't go," I said.

"Go where?" he said.

I wanted to talk but there was no air and his face was close and his eyes were too, and Gran was ashes and Pa was earth and I leaned in crazed and started sniffing his neck, then I put my mouth on his hair and the smell of him got in my mouth and I knew things were falling apart but he didn't back away. Jerky put his hand on the back of my neck and squeezed hard, then I inched my mouth back down and got at his cheek and chewed on it and he pulled back to look at me. Then he kissed me. He got at my mouth and there was nothing left, only a long-ago-knowed taste of him and then he was pushing me down and got on me, straddling, and I grabbed hard to his back, then ran my hand down his leg and we started rolling and yanking, tasting and flying. He stuck my hand in his mouth and I tore at his coat and shirt and put my mouth on his chest, and straw got on my lips. He tugged at my coat, pants, long johns, his hands everywhere, my hands everywhere and I was sweating in the cold and tasting a sweetness I never knew and he bit my ear and said my name and we bucked and shuddered riding like one, this time ours forever.

After, we lay there brushing the straw off of us. We didn't talk. Then I remembered. "Ma's sister got a job for me in New York City, working horses," I said. "Tomorrow she leaves. I could be rich I reckon."

We lay still and the cork holes and cracks in the barn wood started to change color, taking on that dawn glow. Time was running out.

"Hell Bud you can't pass that up," he said.

"But we're going west," I said.

He was quiet. A cock crowed. His Ma would be up soon fetching eggs.

"You come back with a barrel of money, and we can ride out west in style," Jerky said.

I lay there knowing I had to get up. We had to move out of the barn, into the daylight. I knew that, but I wished we didn't. I wished we never had to move at all.

18

A strange frosty morning mist came up, rising from some far-off valley I figured, maybe down by the iced-over Beaver Lake where the blue light bluffs rise with hard cut caves hiding dark things. I was at the door looking out, that shiny black car circled by the mist, only the top of it showing, like it was sinking and would disappear soon. The car was loaded full since dawn. The Hughes fella was taking that prize horse down to Louisiana where it would be loaded on the ocean boat headed for New York City.

Ma had tried to hold strong but ran off to her room after a whole lot of hugging with Gert and promises and whispering. Mr. Nadir was hanging out in front of the jalopy, smoking. He seemed like he'd been ready to leave about half a minute after he arrived. I felt something behind me, wishing it was Gran or Pa and the crazy mist had dragged them both from the grave. But before I turned I knew it was only Gert. Gran's voice was gone again, and things dark and spooked had lost their voice to me, and as much as I'd feared all that, I missed it.

"All right, Bud," she said.

She stepped past me, then turned back. She reached out her hand. She wasn't wearing a glove. She had a man's hand, with knuckles big and hard as walnuts.

"Good luck," she said.

I took her hand and she gave me a long solid shake, then she turned on her heel and moved fast into that mist. There was a racket, that machine starting up, and then it was gone.

Everything went still for a long while after that. I didn't even hear the birds, nor Ma's whimpering. I sat on the front porch despite the cold and stared at the mist, knowing, just knowing. From the barn, I heard Lightning neigh and I knew he knew too.

And sure enough, from down the road, climbing up our hill to the house, taking his time, was Jerky. He and I was gonna take a long walk around the property and see what it all was fit for. Because after all, we were farmers, not cowboys. The two of us were of the earth.

CPSIA information can be obtained
at www.ICGtesting.com
Printed in the USA
BVHW031000100721
611457BV00032B/399